SCARECROW

SCARE

THOMAS DUNNE BOOKS
ST. MARTIN'S MINOTAUR ⚞ NEW YORK

CROW

ROBIN HATHAWAY

THOMAS DUNNE BOOKS.
An imprint of St. Martin's Press.

www.minotaurbooks.com

Book design by Nick Wunder

Library of Congress Cataloging-in-Publication Data

Hathaway, Robin.
    Scarecrow / Robin Hathaway.—1st ed.
      p. cm.
    ISBN 0-312-30851-5
    1. Women physicians—Fiction. 2. Migrant agricultural laborers—Crimes against—Fiction. 3. New Jersey—Fiction. I. Title.

PS3558.A7475 S28   2003
813'.54—dc21

                                       2002024532

10 9 8 7 6 5 4 3 2

To my brother, Jack—with love

ACKNOWLEDGMENTS

As always, I am deeply grateful to my editor, Ruth Cavin; to my agent, Laura Langlie; to my doctor-husband, Bob; to my daughters, Julie and Anne, and my son-in-law, Jason, for their tireless help and loyal support.

The idea for Jo Banks, the motel doctor, came to me one evening at the kitchen table while talking to Bob over a few beers. She began to really come to life as the foam settled on the third (or was it the fourth?). I don't usually resort to drink for inspiration, but every now and then it activates those tired brain cells, loosens those creative juices. Hey, now they even say beer is good for your health! A beer a day keeps the doctor away? Well, not in this case. In this case, the beer brought the doctor right to my door.

Jo Banks and Andrew Fenimore, the hero of my other series, are both in the medical profession, but they are very different. Fenimore, a middle-aged cardiologist of the old school, practices solo from his townhouse in Philadelphia and still makes house calls. On his days off, instead of heading for the golf course, he solves crimes. Jo, a modern, twenty-something family practitioner, provides medical services to motel guests and employees—most motels have a doctor on call—and makes her doctor visits on a motorcycle. If a crime happens to come her way, which it often does, she is more than happy to tackle it.

Besides sleuthing, these two doctors have something else in common: They both prize their independence and refuse to become slaves to "the establishment."

I hope you'll enjoy Dr. Banks as much as Dr. Fenimore. Who knows, maybe one day their paths will cross! At a medical convention, perhaps? What a perfect spot for a murder. They may even compete to see who solves the crime first. (Always thinking!)

"Good-day," said the Scarecrow, in a rather husky voice.

"Did you speak?" asked the girl, in wonder.

"Certainly," answered the Scarecrow; "how do you do?"

"I'm pretty well, thank you," replied Dorothy, politely; "how do you do?"

"I'm not feeling well," said the Scarecrow, with a smile, "for it is very tedious being perched up here night and day to scare away crows."

"Can't you get down?" asked Dorothy.

"No, for this pole is stuck up my back. If you will please take away the pole, I shall be greatly obliged to you."

Dorothy reached up both arms and lifted the figure off the pole; for, being stuffed with straw, it was quite light.

"Thank you very much," said the Scarecrow, when he had been set down on the ground. "I feel like a new man."

—from *The Wizard of Oz*

SCARECROW

PROLOGUE

It was one of those freakish October days when the mercury shoots up to the nineties, catching everyone off guard. It caught the Potter boys off guard. They'd taken the day off from their jobs at the tomato cannery to go hunting—all togged out in their bright orange down vests. They look like three pumpkins, thought their mother fondly, as she watched them heading down the road.

But by ten o'clock, they were stripped to the waist and spending more time sweating than shooting.

"Aw, let's get some beer," Jake said.

"I ain't fired a shot yet!" whined Willard.

"Take some shots at them crows," Oscar suggested.

Willard obliged. *Bam!*

Plop. The bird landed at his feet. Grinning, he stepped delicately over it.

"Let's shake up Farmer Perkins's scarecrow." Jake was not about to be outdone by his younger brother. Taking aim, he fired. *Bam!* Its hat flew off.

"Holy moley!" Oscar cried.

"Perkins'll have your hide for that," Willard mumbled.

Sure enough, a man was heading into the field, brandishing something.

Jake ran as fast as his beer belly would let him, to the base of

the scarecrow. He bent to retrieve the hat. But to his brothers'
astonishment, he didn't pick it up. He just stayed there, bent over.
The brothers looked at each other. Farmer Perkins was gaining
ground. And now they could see what he was carrying. A horse
whip.

The boys ran to their brother's aid.

"What the hell?" Willard puffed, as he came up.

Oscar fixed Jake with his *you asshole!* stare.

Wordlessly, Jake pointed to the scarecrow's left pant leg.

A bare foot protruded from it.

CHAPTER 1

When I hit the Jersey Turnpike, I went into autopilot and the windshield fogged up with scenes I'd just as well forget.

The door to my office opened without a warning knock. I glanced up from the JAMA article I was reading. "What is it, Sue?"

My secretary hesitated, then blurted, "Sophie Miller . . . that little red-haired girl . . ."

"Yes?"

"She's . . . gone."

"What?" I sat upright.

"That viral infection . . . it was spinal meningitis."

My heart contracted and my mouth went dry as my body registered the news.

"The nurse just called. They want you to come over to the hospital and talk to the parents."

OhmygodOhmygodOhmygod.

"Can I do anything?" Sue stayed in the doorway.

I shook my head.

The door closed.

I placed my face in my hands.

I swerved, narrowly missing the red sports car that dove in front of me. I concentrated on the stream of trucks and cars ahead.

"So that's why you're leaving. . . ." Ken's lower lip protruded from

his beard, a sure sign he was beginning one of his famous sulks.

I continued throwing things in my backpack.

"It wasn't your fault!" he shouted.

"I should have been sharper," I said in a dull tone.

"You can't win 'em all."

"You didn't see those parents."

"It was your first time," he said. "You'll get used to it."

I looked at him.

He lowered his eyes.

Turning, I went back to my packing.

"Hey, I know it was tough." He came up behind me and tried to give me a hug.

I shrugged him off.

"I'm going for a walk," he said in an injured tone.

I zipped toothbrush, toothpaste, and deodorant into an outside pocket.

The door closed.

"When you get back," I muttered to the empty room, "I'll be outta here."

The deep nasal blast of a horn caused me to glance in the rearview mirror. A tractor trailer—huge, bloodthirsty beast—was bearing down on me. In fact, the road behind me was jam-packed with bloodthirsty beasts—wild boars, rhinos, wolves, jackals—all riding my tail. All out to get me. I pressed the accelerator of my Budget Rent-a-Car.

"I'll only be gone a few days." I pulled on the phone wire, watching it stretch and recurl.

"You and Ken have a blowup?"

"None of your business."

Silence.

"Sorry, Dad. I'm on edge. I'll call you when I get there."

"And where, may I ask, is 'there'?"

He only spoke formally when he was angry—or hurt.

Suddenly I realized I had planned everything except my destination. "I'll let you know when I get there. Bye, Dad."

The gang behind me had thinned out. I automatically reached

in the side pocket for a CD. Empty. *Damn.* In my rush to get out of the apartment, I'd left my CDs behind.

I turned on the radio. Talk show on capital punishment. Should we or shouldn't we? *Flick.* Sinatra crooning fifties love songs. *Flick.* Fire and brimstone from a Bible Belt preacher. *Flick.* "Ninety degree temperatures break record for October"—followed by a heated discussion on global warming. *Flick.* Back to capital punishment. The emcee—against it. His caller—for it: "The obvious answer to prison overcrowding."

> We interrupt this program to bring you an important news bulletin: An unidentified body was found this morning in Bayfield, New Jersey. At ten-thirty A.M., Jake Potter was walking with his brothers in a cornfield when he stumbled on the body. Disguised as a scarecrow, it was hanging from a crossbeam in the middle of the field. Jake would have walked right by if he hadn't stooped to pick up something and caught sight of a bare foot dangling from the pant leg. "Scared the bejeesus outta me," Jake said—

I punched OFF and concentrated on the road. It took more than a single dead body to hold the attention of a Manhattanite. The rhythm of the traffic combined with the monotony of the scenery had a soporific effect. Twice I caught myself about to doze off. Coffee time. I looked for the next service plaza.

With some caffeine inside me and some more in a cup next to me, I felt better. Sharper. Able to tackle anything. Well, at least to decide where I was going to spend the night.

A sign warned of an approaching toll: LAST EXIT BEFORE BRIDGE. What bridge? DELAWARE MEMORIAL BRIDGE, snapped the next sign.

I didn't want to go to Delaware. I wanted to go to the shore. To the sea. The happiest times of my life had been spent at the seashore. My dad had always rented a cottage for the two of us on our summer vacations. Of course, October wasn't the best time for the shore. Or was it? No swimming, but no crowds either. I swerved onto the exit ramp in the nick of time.

"Thank you, ma'am." He dropped the change into my hand and smiled.

Ma'am? Where had he been? Or, rather, where the hell was I?

The soap-opera scenes of my life petered out along with the Turnpike. When I tried to resurrect them, they flickered and died like an old film. The windshield was clear and what I saw through it made me sit up and take notice. Golden fields topped by a band of indigo sky. The serene line of the horizon broken only by an occasional lone tree or scarecrow.

Scarecrow?

I slowed down. What a beautiful specimen! The first one I'd ever seen outside of *the Wizard of Oz*. And my rearview mirror was empty. That pack of jungle beasts must have opted for Delaware. In fact, I was the only car on the road. As I drove, the sky blushed crimson, turning the fields blood red. Fields and sky. Sky and fields. I don't know how long I drove. When the sky cooled to lavender and the fields to deep purple, I turned on my headlights. The beams picked out signs of civilization. (If that's what you call it.) A used-car lot, Harry's Bar and Grill, and a motel with an orange neon sign—OAKVIEW MOTOR LODGE. And below it: LO R TES. It was the customer's job to fill in the blanks. If I hadn't been exhausted, I would have driven on to look for more upscale lodgings. (None of my colleagues would have been caught dead in this fleabag.) But not long ago I had been a lowly intern, up to my ears in debt, and I had often stayed in such places—when I could afford to travel at all. Besides, it gave me a kick to stay where my pretentious colleagues wouldn't be caught dead. I turned into the parking lot and was faced with the movie set for *It Happened One Night*. Three wooden cabins all in a row, each with two windows and a door with a number fixed to its center: 1, 2, and 3. I looked around expectantly for Clark Gable. No such luck. *It Happened One Night* and *Casablanca* had been my two mainstays when I was a medical student. I couldn't afford much recreation, but I did have a VCR and a few videos. I played those movies over and over. If anyone deserved credit for getting me through medical school (besides Dad) it was Gable and Bogie. And it was a toss-up which one I owed the most.

Cabin number "one" had a light over the door and a small orange neon sign below. OFFICE, it read. For some reason, that little cabin with its warm glowing sign was a comfort—like a bowl of hot broth when you had a bad cold.

I turned off the ignition and went in to register.

CHAPTER 2

The cabin was empty except for a battered desk with a sign propped on it: PLEASE REGISTER IN REAR.

So the three cabins were a stage set. The real motel, located a hundred feet behind, was a double-decker cinderblock structure—a carbon copy of a million other ugly motels around the country. I was too tired to look for another.

When I came in the elderly desk clerk was talking excitedly on the phone. "In Perkins's field. One of the Potter boys . . . ?" He glanced up as I approached the desk. "Gotta customer, Mag. I'll call you back."

As I signed in, the desk clerk looked at me slightly askance. Was it my chic outfit—an Evan Picone suit and sneakers? Or could he possibly disapprove of a young woman traveling alone? Then I remembered; I was in the boondocks. Liberated females were a scarce commodity. Here the women probably still tended the hearth while their mates went out foraging for food.

He glanced at my signature. Jo Banks. "Jo—as in Josephine?"

"No. Jo as in Joe. I was named after my dad."

This silenced the old codger. His own name, PAUL NELSON, was neatly displayed by a sign on his desk. He handed me my key. "Room twenty-one, second floor."

"Thanks."

"If you want to unload your luggage, you can drive your car up to the stairwell in the rear."

"This *is* my luggage," I indicated my backpack.

The man nodded. "I know you youngsters like to travel light." He actually smiled a fatherly smile.

Youngster? I hadn't been called that in years. I smiled back.

He was already reaching for the phone.

Is there anything more depressing than a two-star motel? I pushed open the heavy glass door and was hit by the smell of stale cigarettes and disinfectant. The carpet was clean but an uninspiring shit brown, marred by stains which had defied the most potent detergents. This color was echoed by the walls in a somewhat lighter shade. As I closed the door to my room, I was surprised to find only one lock. Where I came from motels usually provided three, and a chain to boot. Although the desk clerk looked nothing like Norman Bates, I placed a chair under the doorknob before taking a shower. Afterward, I lay down on the bed, planning to take a short nap before finding something to eat.

A scream woke me. My luminous watch dial read 2:15.

I stuck my head into the corridor as someone emerged from the room next door. A young man—obviously upset.

"What's wrong?"

"Lady in room nineteen. Has a bad pain. I'm going for a doctor."

"I'm a doctor." If I hadn't been fuzzy with sleep, I would have kept my mouth shut.

An incredulous expression crossed his face, the one often worn by American males when confronted by a female doctor.

"Honest," I said.

Relief took the place of surprise. "Would you take a look at her?"

"Let me get my stuff. By the way, who are you?"

"Jack, the night clerk."

I turned back to my room and grabbed my medical kit from my backpack. Catching sight of myself in the mirror, I stopped cold. No wonder Jack-the-night-clerk had looked incredulous. In my nightgown (a T-shirt, extra-large), I hardly looked like someone you would want to entrust your health to. I threw on my clothes and went next door.

I saw the man before the woman. He was crouched in a green vinyl chair (an exact replica of the one in my room), chewing on his lip, staring at the woman. The woman was curled in a fetal position in the center of the double bed, moaning softly.

Jack, who had gone in ahead of me, spoke to the man. "This lady's a doctor."

The man looked startled—whether by my sex or by the speed with which I had been produced, I wasn't sure.

The woman didn't look up when I bent over her—all her senses were concentrated on her pain.

"Can you tell me where it hurts?"

She indicated her lower abdomen. As I began to examine her, I noticed a long horizontal scar transecting the two upper quadrants. Gallbladder, probably, and a lousy job, too. No self-respecting American woman would put up with a scar like that. "You've had abdominal surgery. What for?"

She shrugged.

I drew a line across my abdomen with my finger and said again, "What for?"

Another shrug.

Maybe she didn't know the word for gallbladder. I looked at the man. He, too, gave me a blank stare. I let it go. While I took her pulse, she answered my other questions in perfect English with just a trace of an accent that I couldn't place. And why should I? I wasn't exactly a world traveler and languages had never been my thing. No, she had no diarrhea. Yes, she felt nauseous. No, the pain was no better.

"What did you have for dinner?"

"Crab cakes," the man answered for her.

"Does crab usually disagree with her?"

With a sudden motion, the woman rose from the bed and ran for the bathroom. We heard sounds of retching. The man made no move to go to her.

I went to the door. "Are you all right?"

Bent double over the toilet bowl, she didn't answer. I grabbed a towel and handed it to her.

While the man (at my suggestion) helped her into a clean nightgown, I waited outside in the hall. Dismal places, motel corridors—with their rows of identical doors and red exit signs blinking at either end. Like exits to hell. They remind me of bad dreams in which I run down endless corridors toward exits, which are always just out of reach. Deciding I had let enough time elapse, I rapped lightly on the semiclosed door.

The husband pulled the door wide and for the first time, I got a good look at him. Small, pudgy, with a pasty complexion. A Pillsbury doughboy, minus the smile.

"I think she is better." He spoke with the same accent.

We both looked at the woman. She was lying on her back, legs stretched out under the sheet, no longer forced into a circumference by pain. And her color was back.

"How are you feeling?" I asked her.

Her eyes flew open. "Better," she said, after taking a moment to think it over. She closed her eyes again.

I turned to her husband. (I guess he was her husband.) "I think your wife had acute food poisoning. She should have nothing to eat or drink. Only water until morning. If she has any more pain, be sure to call me. I'm right next door. Room twenty-one."

He nodded.

No offer of payment. Not even a thanks. Maybe where he came from health care was included in the accommodations. On my way out I noticed their bags, packed and ready to go, near the door. "It would be best if I see her before you leave in the morning," I said.

As I closed my door, I fervently hoped the woman's pains would not come back. I hadn't treated a patient since Sophie. I had taken a leave of absence. And I wasn't ready to go back. Not yet. Answering that night call had been a reflex—the result of having been awakened from a deep sleep.

I was still tired. Returning to my own room was like returning to an old friend.

My last thought as I dozed off was of my neighbors' bathroom. When I had looked in, it had been empty of the usual bathroom clutter. No toothpaste, shampoo, or shaver. And the midget bar of soap had lain on the sink, still wrapped. Either my neighbors were unacquainted with personal hygiene, or about to make a hasty departure.

Wait. There had been one personal object—an open box of prunes on the back of the toilet. Did one of them suffer from constipation? That was one of the troubles with being a doctor—your mind never strayed far from the bodily functions.

CHAPTER 3

Pale bars of sunlight striped the acid green blanket. When I had pulled the psychedelic orange bedspread back the night before, I had hoped something more appealing would show up underneath. No such luck. I stretched my legs and for the first time in months did not run into a masculine calf on my left. I wasn't sure if I missed it or was glad of my new freedom. Plenty of time to sort that out later. I jumped up and went into the bathroom. As I brushed my teeth I thought of my next-door neighbors. All was eerily quiet from that direction. No voices, human or TV. What time was it? I checked my watch. Eight o'clock. I wondered if I should make a house call on my new patient. Decided against it. Doctors weren't supposed to pursue their clients (especially when no fee was involved).

I trotted down the corridor toward the smell of coffee like a hound dog after a scent. The mixture I'd made in my room (instant coffee and warm tap water—the recipe that had gotten me through med school) hadn't done the trick. My eyelids were lead-lined. My brain—on hold. The scent was coming from the lobby, the name I generously bestowed on a cramped room furnished with a vinyl sofa, two vinyl chairs, and a card table. This morning the table was covered with a paper cloth, a coffee pot, Styrofoam cups, plastic spoons, and a paper plate piled high with store-bought doughnuts.

A motley group hovered around the table, sipping and munching, eyeing each other awkwardly. My neighbors from the night before were not among them. I grabbed a Styrofoam cup, squirted some coffee into it, cadged a doughnut, and went to pay my bill. My fatherly friend, Mr. Nelson, was back at his post.

"Hi," I said.

He looked up from his paper. " 'Morning. Sleep well?"

Did I detect a twinkle? "Ah—" I stammered.

"What is your fee?"

I stood dumbly. I had yet to acquire the business acumen of most of my colleagues.

"Would a free night's lodging cover it?"

"Sure."

"Done," he said. "And—thank you."

I couldn't contain my curiosity. "Have they left?"

"The Milacs? Yes. Skipped out before breakfast in a blue Ford Taurus."

"Without paying?"

He nodded.

So I was right. "They ripped us both off."

"Yep."

"Did you get their license number?"

"They had temporary plates."

"Did you call the police?"

"They'll be out of the county by now, and they're too small potatoes for the state police." He folded his paper and laid it aside. "Do you do much of this?"

My mind was still on the Milacs. "Doctoring?"

"At motels, I mean?"

"It's not my normal beat." I laughed.

"Which is?"

"Group practice. Hospital based."

"And you like that?"

I shrugged.

"From time to time we have emergencies like the one last night. It's hard to get a doctor. . . ."

I thought I was pretty quick, but he'd lost me.

"Oh, I know you couldn't make a living from one motel," he said. "But most motel owners like to have a doctor to call on in emergencies." He was warming to his theme. "And there are quite a few motels in this area. If you served them all together, plus some local patients . . ."

He *had* to be kidding.

"It's a nice place to live—South Jersey," he rambled on. "Pretty. And quiet. Where are you from?"

I found my voice. "Manhattan."

"Ah—I guess you would find us a little dull." He sounded genuinely disappointed.

Motel doctor? What a hare-brained idea. "Well, thanks for the bed and breakfast." I returned the key. "Oh." I turned back. "Could you direct me to the nearest seashore?"

"There's no 'sea' around here. Just the bay."

"The bayshore, then."

He pulled a map from his desk drawer and with an arthritis swollen finger traced the nearest route to the Delaware Bay. It looked almost as big as the ocean. "Here, take it." He handed me the map. "It's easy to get lost around here. The biggest landmark is the cooling tower of the nuclear power plant, about five miles from here. You can't miss it. Better take an extra doughnut just in case."

He really was a nice old codger. I grabbed the doughnut and shot him a farewell grin.

CHAPTER 4

I was thoughtful as I drove out of the parking lot. I'd never treated a pair of crooks before. At least, not that I knew of. When I was an intern at Bellevue, I'd treated everything that came in the door, but I wasn't instructed to inquire into their professions.

The Oakview Motor Lodge was the first in a long line of seedy commercial establishments—gas stations, trailer parks, used-car lots, and bars. I was eager to get back to the beautiful scenery of yesterday, but it was a two-lane highway and the pickup truck in front of me full of rednecks in hunting attire was in no hurry. I was crawling along at forty-five when I spotted the girl. A child, really. Skinny, in tight jeans with barely formed breasts under her T-shirt. She had a backpack like mine. The idiot was trying to hitch a ride. The pickup slowed down. So did I. It'd be better if she took one from me than from that bunch. I was convinced deer wasn't the only thing on their list of fair game.

"Hop in." Close-up the girl looked about thirteen. Frizzy red hair and so many freckles they blurred into a tan smudge over the bridge of her nose. "Where you headed?"

"New York."

"New York?" I repeated, as if I'd never heard of the place.

She didn't say anything.

"Well, you're headed in the wrong direction," I said. "I just came from there."

"Oh." Her hand found the door handle.

"Don't," I spoke sharply, pulling onto the shoulder. I placed a restraining hand on her arm. "Aren't you a bit young to be taking off for New York alone?"

She shrugged off my hand and pressed the door handle down.

"Wait . . ." She was already out and loping down the road toward New York. I could have made a U-turn; there wasn't another car in sight. But what was the point? She would never get into my car again voluntarily, and if I forced her I could be accused of kidnapping. Instead, I drove into the first gas station. I parked to one side and approached the attendant. "What's the number of the state police?"

"Trouble?"

"A kid down the road—trying to hitch a ride. Could be a runaway."

He shrugged. "Kids hitch rides around here all the time. It's perfectly safe. You a stranger here?"

I ignored the question. "She told me she was headed for New York."

He scratched his head. "That's different. Use my office phone." He gave me the number.

"By the way—" I turned back. "—what's this place called?"

"Polecat Corner."

I blinked, but he seemed to see nothing peculiar in the name.

I went to make my call. After I'd hung up, I felt like a stool pigeon. What if she was running away from something worse than what she was running toward? Child abuse wasn't confined to urban areas.

Back on the road, I thought about the people I'd met during my first twenty-four hours in the boondocks. A pair of larcenists and a runaway. Quite a record—even for a jaded New Yorker.

CHAPTER 5

At the end of a muddy road with more potholes than a Manhattan side street, I slurped to a stop and stepped out into the three inches of mud that hadn't made it to my windshield. Damn. My brand-new Reeboks! Well, the damage was done.

The bay was clean and bright, stretching to a pale gray line that I guessed was the state of Delaware. I kept on walking to the bay's edge. There, the mud turned into sand like brown sugar and the water lapped gently over my sneakers. I shut my eyes and took a deep breath. Salt. The sun felt warm on my eyelids. I was a kid again—lugging buckets of sand, tearing down the beach, my feet slapping against the wet sand, wading into the water, jumping the waves, being knocked down by a wave, my mouth full of sand. (It didn't taste like brown sugar.) The squawk of a seagull. I opened my eyes. Perched on a piling, crusty with barnacles, he stared at me. Looking for a handout, no doubt. "Sorry, buster." I held out my empty hands. He turned his head away, unaware that he had ruined my reverie of innocent childhood.

Hey, I was no child.

I was an almost-thirty-year-old woman running away from the flotsam and jetsam of a botched career and a tired love affair. Shit. Where had that popped up from? People didn't have love affairs anymore. They had relationships. I kicked a beer can. People even

managed to desecrate this remote paradise with their dirty drop-
pings. I looked up with a glare, as if hoping to find the culprit. But
there was no one in sight.

A rotting log lay half-in, half-out of the water. I sat on the
half-out end. After a few minutes, I pulled off my sneakers and
socks and moved to the half-in end. For a while I played in the
water with my toes, making tiny amber waves. It was warm for
October. Indian summer. The sun felt good on my back. Chin in
hand, my eyelids began to droop. I don't know how long I dozed
there, but when I opened my eyes my toes were wrinkled. *What's
wrong with you? Beginning a case of Chronic Fatigue Syndrome?* I dried
my feet with a sock and pulled on my sneakers. Time to start back.
Back? To what? That mangy motel? That poor old caretaker would
think I'd changed my mind and was taking him up on his offer.

Motel doctor.

My guffaw flushed a brown, spindly-legged bird out of the
reeds. Catching sight of me, he darted back again. One last look at
the bay. I had to shield my eyes against its brassy glare. Hunger
pangs told me it must be well past noon. I got in the car and
reached for my sunglasses. Wonder if they found that girl? A
twinge of guilt. Torn between the girl who wanted to get away
and whoever might be worried about her at home. I must be getting old. A few years ago I would have thought of only the girl. I
maneuvered the car through a muddy U-turn. My fenders were
iced with mud an inch thick. Budget-Rent-a-Car would love me.
Feathery reeds caressed the car on either side. Now and then a red-
winged blackbird (one of the few birds I knew) darted in front of
me. I rounded a bend and slammed on the brakes.

In the middle of the road stood a man poised with a bow and
arrow. The arrow wasn't aimed at me, but still . . . I leaned out the
window. "Yo, Robin Hood!"

He put the arrow away and stalked toward me, spewing anger
like exhaust from a tailpipe. When he drew near he said, "You just
scared off the whole herd. I've been waiting all morning."

"Sorry." Although I wasn't. I liked deer.

"What're you doing here?"

"Is this a private road?" I swiveled my head. "I don't see any sign."

"There hasn't been a sign for years, but everybody knows. . . . Where you from?"

"New York."

His face closed up.

"New Yorkers aren't a popular brand around here, huh?"

"Don't know any."

"And don't want to."

"I don't want people pokin' around . . ."

"Is there something sacred about that mud puddle I just visited?" Now *I* was getting hot under the collar.

He looked at my car for the first time. "I can direct you to a nice car wash."

I looked over his shoulder at the field where the herd must have been. It was the color of butter. A bundle of clouds like a pile of freshly mashed potatoes sailed above it. It was as quiet as a church on Monday. My anger melted. "I can see why you want to protect this." I gestured at the field. "I won't hand out any travel brochures when I get back to Manhattan."

He smiled. It changed him—like that dab of red on a blackbird's wing in the spring, from something ordinary to something extraordinary. "Sorry," he said. "I didn't mean to be unfriendly."

"No?" I eyed his bow. "I better be going."

He stepped aside.

I looked back once in the rearview mirror. He was looking after me.

CHAPTER 6

South Jersey isn't overpopulated with fast-food places. I passed a roadside stand piled with pumpkins, apples, jugs of cider, and a few squash. Beggars can't be choosers. I backed up and stopped. No one in sight. A bunch of plastic bags hung from the roof of the wooden shed and there was a jar with a hand-penciled sign stuck to it: WHEN I'M NOT HERE, GOD IS WATCHING. I thought how that would go over in the stalls on Third Avenue. I bagged three apples, picked up a jug of cider, and toyed with the idea of a pumpkin. But where to put it? In the rear window of the car? A skinny woman in an apron was making her way toward me from the farmhouse.

"Nice day," she said, coming up. "You're not from around here."

Was I wearing a sign?

"I noticed your plates."

They didn't miss a trick in this neighborhood. I'd hate to be on the lam like my neighbors from last night. I wouldn't stand a chance. "I'm looking for a place to eat," I said.

She frowned. "Nothing around here. You'd have to get back to the main road."

"And where is that?"

"Wait a minute." She smoothed the apron over her lean front.

"There is Lester's." She looked down the road, running a bony hand through her hair. "It's behind the country store on Snakeskin Road. The boys go there for a bite when they're done hunting."

I could just see the boys lined up at the counter, their red necks glowing, swilling beer and munching venison burgers. "Thanks. I'll find something." I took off with a wave.

By four-thirty, I still hadn't eaten. My stomach was rumbling like a bowling alley on a Saturday night. And rush hour was starting up. There were at least three other cars on the road besides mine. One driver was in such a hurry to get home, he actually passed me. To my left loomed the cooling tower of the nuclear power plant. It had to be that. A giant chimney, black against the crimson sky, spewing clouds of steam. Flashing lights circled its gaping mouth, warning airplanes to keep away. Suddenly, I felt for those Pompeiians who had lived their short lives in the shadow of Vesuvius. What had Mr. Nelson said? "The biggest landmark . . . five miles from here." A glance at the map revealed the sad truth. I had been traveling in a circle. After driving all day, I was only five miles from the Oakview Motor Lodge. I turned down yet another nameless country road (they didn't believe in road signs in South Jersey) and tried to decide what to do. The crimson sky had turned a deep plum. The headlights of some cars were already glowing. I was sick of driving. Hungry and thirsty. I was contemplating a juicy hamburger and a frosty Budweiser when a noise in my right ear nearly sent me off my seat. I pulled over and bumped to a halt. A blowout. In the middle of nowhere. Just as it was getting dark. Great. I looked around. Of course I had to pick the most deserted spot I'd been in all day. Not a house or a barn in sight. On one side lay a field of charred cornstalks; on the other, an empty field edged by a dark wood. Wait a minute, there's someone . . . oh, shit. Not a helpful farmer. Just another scarecrow.

At least I didn't have to worry about car-jackers here. And thank God dad had taught me how to change a tire. He might make fun of the feminist movement, but he didn't want his daughter caught helpless on the road, either. With a sigh, I opened the trunk, took out the spare (one of those useless doughnuts), and fumbled for the jack.

I had just gotten the tire raised and was tackling the nuts when I was blinded by headlight beams. A car coming. I was well off the road with my blinkers on, so I wasn't worried. When the car drew near, it slowed, as if the driver was debating whether to stop and offer help. He sped on. Out of the corner of my eye, I glimpsed temporary plates. Didn't that crook couple have temporary plates? I went back to the tire.

Once the tire was changed, I still had the problem of being lost. I poked along cautiously. I had no faith in those doughnuts. My gas gauge was also making me nervous. I turned into the first driveway I came to. Poor choice. Deeply rutted, it was bad for the baby tire. At the end I could make out a farmhouse. Its bare wood glinted silver in the first rays of a full moon. A big, ugly dog barked ferociously. I didn't dare get out of the car. I'd handled a couple of rabies cases at Bellevue and I wasn't about to become one. I sat in the car and waited. After a few minutes the screen door banged open and a man emerged, shouting at the dog. I waited until I was sure he had a good grip on the dog's collar before I got out of the car.

He shoved the dog inside the screened porch and came toward me.

"Could you direct me to the Oakview Motor Lodge?" The words surprised me as soon as they were out of my mouth.

"Stranger?" He was the first person I'd met who didn't make *stranger* sound like *skunk cabbage*.

"Yes, but I have a map." I handed him Mr. Nelson's map, and in the glow of my headlights he traced my route. Just as I thought, the motel was only a couple of miles away. I'd traveled all day to end up where I started. "Thanks," I said.

"My pleasure."

I looked at him closely. Having taken him for a farmer, I was surprised by his crisp, cultured voice with a touch of a European accent—not the soft country drawl of the natives around there.

"Juri!" A guttural voice croaked from the dark recesses of the porch. It was impossible to tell its sex. "Who's there?"

"A young woman. She's lost."

"Well, send her away." A window banged shut.

"Thanks again," I said, and smiled my most engaging smile. He didn't respond. I guess he couldn't see it in the dark.

I dropped the car off at the gas station where I'd made my phone call that morning. Mike (his name was sewn across the pocket of his jumpsuit) greeted me like an old friend.

"Did they catch up with that girl?"

"I don't know." I shrugged.

He promised to replace the tire early the next morning. It was a half-mile walk from the garage to the motel. On the way, in desperation, I detoured into the sleazy-looking dive called Harry's Bar & Grill. It was the grill I was interested in. The hamburger wasn't bad, but the stares and side-looks from the male clientele did nothing to improve it. I ate quickly and left, having gotten the message: Women in South Jersey do not frequent bars to satisfy their hunger—at least, not my kind of hunger.

Mr. Nelson was just packing up for the night when I walked in. He was talking in low tones to Jack-the-night-clerk who was hovering, waiting to take over. They stopped talking immediately, registered surprise, then grinned. It was a good feeling.

"Any vacancies?" I asked, although the orange vacancy sign had been aglow when I came in.

"For you? We'll make up the bridal suite," Mr. Nelson said. Jack let out a hoot.

"A simple single will do," I muttered, feeling a blush begin.

"How about number twenty-one?" He reached for the key.

"Fine." Really like coming home. As I left, they were both still wearing those foolish grins.

CHAPTER 7

When I entered my room, the first thing I did was stash away the Bible, so kindly provided by the Gideon Society. I didn't want to be reminded of my sins every time I walked in the door. Next, I stripped the bed down to the sheets and shoved the ugly orange bedspread and the acid green blanket out of sight in a drawer. In the acre-wide mirror over the bureau, I confronted my reflection.

What the hell are you doing?

Making myself at home.

Why?

No answer.

In this state of mind I went to bed. But, unlike the night before, I couldn't sleep. Tossing and turning, at one point I had to quell an impulse to retrieve the Bible. I was that desperate. Shortly after this, I fell into a restless, dream-ridden sleep. I was running down endless corridors, like the one outside my door, with Ken either ahead of me—just out of reach, or behind me—closing in on me.

At some point the scene changed. I was in a pristine modern medical complex where I shared an office the size of a small supermarket with ten other doctors. I sat huddled in my cubicle, waiting for a patient to call. The other doctors shuffled back and forth in the hall outside the door, clucking and muttering. The only words I could make out were my name: "Dr. Banks"—cluck, cluck. "Dr. Banks"—mutter, mutter. When I woke up I was wrestling my pillow.

I dozed off again. This time I was walking down a hospital corridor. A middle-aged couple was huddled against the wall, clinging to each other. As I approached, the man raised his head. His eyes, red from weeping, were accusing, then turned to stone. I woke up shivering.

A dirty dawn was beginning over the parking lot. I had forgotten to pull the drapes. I snapped them shut and turned on the bedside lamp. Instantly the room was cozier. Without the ugly bedclothes, it was halfway habitable. A few pictures, an easy chair, a nice comforter, and the place would be almost homey. I left the light on and snuggled under the sheets. This time I fell into a deep and dreamless sleep.

CHAPTER 8

"*Que hora es, Maria?*"

"*Son las siete y veinte.*"

I woke to the sound of girlish voices chattering in Spanish outside my door. I peeked out. Two young women in identical gray uniforms gossiped over a metal cart with wheels. The cart was stacked with snowy towels and sprouted a collection of brightly colored cleaning containers. The first girl was leaning on the cart, the second on a mop. Absorbed in their conversation, they didn't notice me. They kept repeating one word over and over in excited tones. "*Espantapajaros!*" I made a mental note to look it up the next time I was near a Spanish dictionary. I closed the door.

Feeling surprisingly rested, I took a quick shower and put on the last of my clean clothes. Underwear, T-shirt, socks. My jeans had seen better days. The bottoms were muddy from yesterday's excursion to the bay. I rolled them up one turn. My Reeboks were hopeless. I used my nail file to chip off the worst of the dried mud and wiped the rest away with a damp towel. Running a hand through my short-cropped hair completed my toilet. As I left my room, the cart was occupying the same spot as before and the girls were still talking. But this time they smiled at me and one of them said, "Good morning."

The smell of coffee was as enticing as the previous morning, but it was after eight o'clock and I was in a hurry. I wanted to get my car. I felt uneasy in a strange place without wheels. I bypassed the lobby and ducked out the side door.

The unpromising dawn had turned into a perfect day. Blue sky, fluffy clouds, temperature in the fifties. I set off at a brisk pace. There was something about the air here. Could it be that it was clean? Of course, there was that nuclear plant. But that didn't give off anything noxious—unless it leaked. Happy thought. Was that why this area was so underpopulated? A shrill whistle interrupted these depressing notions. I glanced up in time to see a mud-spattered pickup truck with three goons in the front seat. Uh-oh, they were pulling off up ahead, waiting to ambush me. Shit. If I crossed the road or turned back, I'd look chicken. Oh, what the hell. A seasoned Manhattanite was a match for three country bumpkins. I lifted my chin, looked straight ahead, and strode forward purposefully.

"Hey, beautiful." The driver leaned out.

Not only rude, but a liar.

"Want a lift?"

Coolly, I surveyed him, his two passengers, and his truck. The three goons filled the cab completely, and the back was taken up with a sloppy brown dog and something lumpy under a tarpaulin. "Where? On the roof?"

"Hey," he said, laughing in the direction of his buddies. "She's gotta sense of humor." He turned back to me. "One of these two will give up his seat." He winked. "They'd be glad to."

"No thanks. I need the exercise." I marched on.

They cruised beside me for a while, hurling catcalls. When I didn't react they grew bored and drove on. As they passed, the one next to the window called out, "Party poop!"

As I entered the gas station, Mike dropped whatever he was doing under someone's hood and came right over.

"Did you find what caused my flat?" I asked.

He gave me a peculiar look and reached into his pocket. In his open palm lay a metal blob.

I stared. "Is this hunting season?"

"Yeah. Deer hunting. But this was a twenty-two caliber bullet. Nobody would try to kill a deer with that."

"What would they try to kill?"

"Rabbits, squirrels . . ."

"Me?"

He squinted, sizing up my five-foot-nine self. "Nah."

"What kind of gun would use this?"

"A twenty-two." He dropped the metal blob into my hand as casually, as if returning a lost earring.

As he rolled the ruined tire over to my car (Budget-Rent-a-Car would want proof of my adventure), he called over his shoulder, "Where did you get the flat?"

Of course I couldn't tell him. I gave it a try. "Between a field of burnt corn and another field near a dark wood. There was a scarecrow in the second field and a farm house around the bend badly in need of paint . . ."

"The Sheffield place."

I was impressed.

"Where did the shot come from?"

I tried to remember. "From behind me, I think."

"Somebody in the woods, probably." He stowed the tire in the trunk. "A kid after small game. Nothing to worry about. That'll be twenty-five dollars."

"For the work. But what about the new tire?"

"The tire's not exactly new. I happened to have one lying around and it has a few miles on it. But it'll get you back to New York. No use giving that rental place a brand-new one."

I dug two twenties out of my jeans. While he made the change, I said, "You own this place." It was a statement.

"How'd you know?"

"My dad's a sole proprietor. You remind me of him."

"Not as old, I hope." He grinned.

I laughed.

"What's he do?"

"He's a printer."

An impatient customer tooted the horn at the pump. In Jersey it's all full-serve. "Don't take any wooden bullets," Mike cracked, looking as if he'd said something extremely witty.

I watched him hurry over to the pump to serve a blue Ford Taurus with temporary plates. My gaze flashed to the front seat. A couple. The backs of their heads were vaguely familiar. I was out of the car, pounding toward them. The driver turned. The grim doughboy. As I came puffing up, he started the motor with a jerk. Mrs. Doughboy almost hit the windshield. "Hey!" I reached for the door handle in a futile attempt to hold the car. It slipped from under my hand and bumped over the curb onto the road, leaving the gas hose flopping and leaking on the cement.

"What the hell?" Mike picked up the hose and stood gaping.

No time to explain. I ran back to my car, jumped in, and with a screech of tires I was after them. But they'd had too big a start. After a few miles I gave up and headed back to the motel. On the way I stopped at Mike's and offered to pay for the gas he had been cheated out of.

He refused the money, but demanded, "Friends of yours?"

I told him how we'd met. In the process he learned I was a doctor, but he made no comment.

"I'll keep an eye out for them," he said. "But I guess they won't be coming back here in a hurry."

"Sorry," I said.

"For what? Scaring off two grifters? You did me a favor." He grinned. "By the way, you won't catch me trying to pull anything on you."

"No?"

"No way." He turned back to his business.

CHAPTER 9

I burst into the motel, full of my tale, only to find a stranger at the front desk. A woman.

She looked up. "May I help you?"

"Uh—I was looking for Mr. Nelson."

"Paul had some errands to do. I'm his wife, Maggie."

"I have to talk to him." I was so full of my news I forgot the usual courtesies.

"He should be back soon." She searched my face. "Excuse me, but . . . are you the doctor?"

I focused on her for the first time. Short, plump, gray hair, and gray eyes behind steel-rimmed spectacles. Everything soft, like a toy animal, except the eyes. They were sharp. I nodded.

She reached over the counter and clasped my hand. "He was so grateful for your help the other night. I do hope you're planning to stay on."

"Uh . . ."

"It would be such a comfort to Paul to have someone on hand he could count on. Of course the work would be rewarding for you, too."

Irresistible. Mrs. Santa's charm with a dash of Mary Poppins' starch. "Uh . . ." Had I lost my powers of speech?

"I'll have Paul call you as soon as he comes in. What's your room number?"

"Twenty-one." I was glad to find my vocal chords still worked. As she wrote down the number, I made a hurried exit.

On the way to my room, my stomach registered empty. No breakfast, and it was way past lunchtime. Ever since I'd arrived in South Jersey I had been in a perpetual state of starvation. But I didn't want to leave the motel and miss Mr. Nelson. Two vending machines at the end of my corridor offered a partial solution. Laden with bags of chips and a Coke, I fumbled for the key to my room. No use. Even with one bag clenched in my teeth, I couldn't execute the maneuver. I set the stuff on the floor and noticed the door on my right was open a crack. Someone peered out. A kid. My God—the baby hitchhiker. As soon as I identified her, the door closed.

"Hey!" I rapped on the door.

No answer.

"Yo, come on out and say hello. We met before, remember?"

Still no response.

"Look. We're neighbors. You're not being very neighborly."

Silence.

"How 'bout some Coke and chips? There's a machine down the hall. My treat."

The door reopened—just a crack. She must be hungry.

"Come on in my room."

"I can't," she whispered.

"Why not?"

"I . . . I'm waiting for a friend."

Holy Moses. And I thought New York kids were precocious. "Okay I'll get the stuff and bring it to your room. You'll let me in, right?"

She closed the door and I heard the lock click.

A born optimist, I trotted back to the vending machines and returned laden with enough food, Coke, and ice for ten kids. (Maybe she'd prefer vodka.) As I tried to find a free hand to knock on the door, I spotted another kid, a gangly youth with too much hair, hovering at the end of the hall. He sidled my way, glancing at every room number. When he reached the door next to mine, he paused briefly, gave me and my paraphernalia a dark look, and kept walking. Probably thought I was about to launch a small wedding reception. Now what? Impasse. Should I take all this stuff into my room and invite them both in? Why not? We'd have a party. A lot better than the kind of party he was planning. I knocked on her door. She must have thought it was her Casanova, because she opened up right away.

"Come on to my place. I think your boyfriend's down the hall. Maybe he'd like to join us."

She cast an anxious look down the hall. He was leaning against the fire extinguisher, watching us. She looked back at me, her face an agony of indecision. I solved her dilemma by giving the boy a wave and a yodel.

"I'm having a little party. Come on in."

He came forward reluctantly.

By this time I had gotten my key in the door. I picked up the refreshments and pushed the door open the rest of the way with my rump. There was no rush to follow me in. I dropped the stuff on the bureau and flicked on the radio—a rock station. I turned up the volume to the max, praying there were no guests indulging in an afternoon nap. The music, more than the food, drew them inside. I left the door partially open, feeling like the spider with two flies.

While the kids sat on the enormous bed, snatching awkward glances at each other, I played the heavy hostess. I filled plastic tumblers with ice, poured Coke, passed potato chips around, all the time keeping up a steady stream of cheery, inane chatter:

"I'm really glad you two came by. I'm a stranger in these parts and I was beginning to feel a little lonesome. You know how it is when you're from out of town. It gets boring talking to yourself, eating by yourself." (I almost said, sleeping by yourself.) "Do you live near here? You must, unless you have a car." (All this blather at the top of my lungs, competing with rock at about 110 decibels.) "So . . ." I said and stretched out on what was left of the bed (half a football field), "were you two planning to spend the night?" I had turned the radio down to a level appropriate for someone with only a mild hearing impairment. They couldn't miss my question.

The boy cast a furtive glance at the girl. The girl looked at me and shook her head.

"The afternoon, then?" I asked brightly, crunching on a chip. (God, would I ever get a square meal?) "They have special rates, I hear."

"Where'd you hear that?" the boy blurted.

"Oh, I get around." I let them reflect on that while I refilled their glasses. "You know what?" I said suddenly. "This is dumb. It's a beautiful day out there. Instead of sitting around this dreary motel, how 'bout if we go for a picnic? I've got a car. We can drive to the bay." Without waiting for an answer, I disposed of the trash and gathered up the remains of the food and drink to take with us.

"But I've already paid—" The boy was obviously upset.

There was no mistaking the girl's expression of relief.

"You can get a refund," I assured him. "Give me the key." I held out my hand to the girl.

She dropped the sweaty key in my palm.

"My name's Jo," I told them on the way to the car. "What're yours?"

"Becca," the girl said.

The boy said nothing, sulking.

"He's Randy," she offered.

What else, I thought.

The two babies sat huddled in separate corners of the back, a yard of seat between them, while I drove. "Nice name—Becca," I said. "I had a friend by that name."

"Where is she now?" She had picked up on the *had*.

"Oh, she moved away. I lost track of her." Actually, she had been killed in a car crash, but there was no point getting into that. "I may be staying down here for a while," I said, surprising myself.

"What'll you do?" The conversation was two-way only. The boy was deep in his sulk.

"I'm a doctor. I might practice around here."

Silence.

"Do you ever go to the shore?" I glanced in the rearview mirror. She was shaking her head. He was staring out the window.

"You've never seen the ocean?"

More shakes.

"Well, next spring I'll take you. That's a promise." *Spring? Are you crazy? What's the idea of making promises you can't keep?*

We drove without talking for about a mile.

"I want out here," Randy spoke suddenly.

We were approaching a crossroad with no signs and not a building in sight.

I slowed down. Before I came to a complete stop, he jumped out of the car. As he loped down the empty road to the right, I glanced at Becca in the rearview mirror. Her face was a mask. "He lives near here," she said shortly.

The picnic was a gloomy affair. The sun had gone under a cloud and our hearts weren't in it. Becca was mourning her boyfriend, and I was exhausted from the effort of wrecking his plans.

"Come on," I said, picking up the trash and stowing it in the car. "I'll take you home."

She got in the front seat this time. At first I took this as a sign she had appreciated my afternoon's work. But on second thought, riding in back probably made her carsick.

CHAPTER 10

Becca directed me to her house. When we came to a road with a field filled with charred cornstalks on one side and an empty field surrounded by a dark wood on the other, I leaned over the steering wheel.

"Turn right at the next driveway," she said.

I was experiencing déjà vu that wasn't déjà vu. I really had been over this rut-filled driveway before and I knew it led to a silver farmhouse. Last night, in fact. But now it was daylight and I could see that the farmhouse wasn't silver. It was ordinary pine wood from which the paint had worn away. The sun had bleached it and the wind had weathered it until it had acquired a special sheen. At night, when the moonlight played on it, it had looked like polished silver. Today, it looked more like tarnished pewter. The gingerbread on the porch was as fragile and faded as antique lace. The real lace curtains hanging in the tall windows on the porch were the color of cream, and the rippled window glass reflecting the last rays of the sun was gold.

The dog, which had seemed so ferocious the night before, pushed open the screen door and ran up to the car to greet Becca. He was a beautiful weimaraner, the same shade of tarnished pewter as the house. Becca greeted him with a big hug. I patted him gingerly. "Nice boy."

"Girl," Becca corrected. "Her name's Elsa."

I squatted and fondled her ears. She rewarded me with a long lick, from my chin to my forehead.

"Down, Elsa." Becca led us both up the porch steps. "Aunt, I'm back." She pronounced *aunt* to rhyme with *haunt*.

A woman in her mid-fifties came to the door. She wore a long black skirt and a colorful silk blouse. A cluster of silver bracelets jangled on one arm. Her hair was gray, cut in a style I'd seen only on Fifth Avenue.

"This is Jo. She's a doctor."

Her aunt smiled and gave my hand a limp, ladylike shake. "It was kind of you to bring Becca home. Please come in." She had a soft, lilting voice with the trace of an accent. "I was just about to have a cocktail. Won't you join me?"

"I'm sort of a mess." I glanced down. My jeans had acquired some new brown stains and my sneakers were muddy from the day's adventures.

"Nonsense. This is the country." She took my arm and drew me inside.

The room she ushered me into was anything but country. The living room had shelves of books that soared to the ceiling. The furniture was old leather in dark shades of red and brown. These pieces rested on a worn Oriental rug. But the lamps were what gave the room its warmth. Converted oil lamps with glass shades— amber, ruby, and emerald. The exterior of the house gave no clue to its interior.

"Juri?" The aunt called. A door opened at the other end of the elegant room. I didn't immediately recognize the man who had given me directions the night before. Tonight, instead of work clothes, he was wearing cream-colored slacks and a dark blue jersey. He came toward us, bearing a tray with a cocktail shaker and two glasses.

"I'm going to change," Becca announced. "I'll have a Coke," she told Juri on her way out. She disappeared through another door and I heard her running up the stairs.

"Sit down, dear. We're having Gibsons, but we have Manhattans or white wine if you prefer."

The whole scene was out of sync. Why was the living room of a rural farmhouse decorated to resemble a New York brownstone in the thirties? I wasn't alive then, of course, but I'd seen those movies. It wasn't just the room and choice of cocktails, but the aunt herself. She seemed to emanate the aura of those old movie stars—Joan Crawford, Bette Davis, Claudette Colbert. And Juri, who last night I had taken for a farmer, tonight appeared in the role of debonair valet/boyfriend.

"White wine would be good," I said. The leather chair I crawled into was unbelievably soft. I imagined spending rainy afternoons there, curled up with a book from one of those shelves. Elsa arranged herself at my feet. Juri brought my wine in a glass etched with delicate flowers. I thanked him. He turned immediately to making a fire in the fireplace—the final touch that would make the room perfect.

Becca's aunt settled in the corner of the sofa nearest me and raised her glass. "To your successful Bayfield practice!"

I stared.

"Oh, news travels fast in these parts. Becca's boyfriend told his mother and she called me just before you arrived."

I took a deep swallow of wine. Not my usual screw-top variety. This one had definitely come with a cork.

"Whatever made you choose Bayfield?" Juri, finished with the fire, looked at me over his Gibson.

"I didn't." I took another deep swallow.

My hosts waited politely.

"I came here by accident, and then one thing led to another . . ." My explanation sounded lame, even to me.

"Where are you from?" asked Juri.

"Manhattan. Well, I grew up in Queens."

"And where did you train?"

"New York Hospital."

"And your specialty?"

"Family medicine."

"Bayfield will be a bit of a comedown for you, won't it?"

"It depends what you mean by come down."

"Well . . ."

His third degree was beginning to irritate me.

"And where will you have your office?"

"That's still to be worked out."

"And your patients?"

I paused. I wasn't about to divulge the whole "motel doctor" scheme, which had sounded crazy to me less than twenty-four hours ago. "That remains to be seen."

"Juri, that'll do." The aunt finally exercised her hostess authority.

Becca appeared in fresh jeans and a pale blue turtleneck. She made a pretty picture stretched out on the rug next to Elsa, until she said sharply, "Where's my Coke?"

"Oh, sorry, Bec." Juri leapt to his feet and went to fetch it.

Why was a teenager giving orders to a man in his fifties?

When Juri returned, he brought a plate of cheese and crackers as well as the Coke. He passed the plate around and I suddenly remembered I was ravenous. The cheese was not supermarket cheddar, but a delicate blend from some far-off, exotic place. "This house is beautiful," I said, steering the conversation away from myself and my personal affairs. "May I ask how long you've lived here?"

"Twenty-two years," the aunt said. "Since my marriage. But my husband's family built the house in the eighteen-twenties."

"That old?"

"In this neighborhood, that's new. Many houses are pre-Revolutionary. Some are owned by descendants of the original families. I'm still considered a newcomer in these parts—especially now that Richard's gone."

Juri cast her a look I couldn't read.

Becca jumped up and took my empty glass. I thought she was going to refill it. Instead she handed it to Juri. "She'd like another," she said.

"No, I think I'd better be getting back."

"Oh, why?" Becca looked at her aunt meaningfully.

"Won't you stay for supper, dear? We don't often have visitors. It's such a treat for us."

My stomach was grumbling and I was sorely tempted. But my father always told me, "Leave while you're still wanted." I didn't want to overstay my welcome. But if dinner was of the same caliber as the cheese and wine, it might be worth sticking around.

"Oh, please stay, Jo." Becca's plea tipped the scale. Was it just that morning I had caught this kid trying to run away from home? What lay beneath the surface of this elegant household that would drive her to such a desperate act? "That would be nice," I heard myself say.

Becca grinned. The aunt smiled the correct smile of a 1930s hostess. Juri left the room with my glass.

We moved to other topics. I was telling them how New York City was thriving despite September 11th when I became conscious of rumblings from above—as if someone was moving furniture. At one point it became so loud, we all glanced at the ceiling.

The aunt frowned. Becca wrinkled her nose. I plowed ahead with statistics on the increasing tourist trade in Manhattan.

Juri returned with my wine, but instead of rejoining us, he headed for the kitchen. Becca began tossing pretzel nuggets to Elsa, who deftly caught them in her mouth.

"Not too many," Juri said over his shoulder. "You'll make her sick."

Becca continued to toss them, as if she were deaf.

"What are you studying at school?" I attempted to distract her.

She cast me the disdainful look my question deserved. "Readin', writin,' 'n' 'rithmetic."

"The local school only provides the basics," the aunt said.

"They don't even have a gym." Becca glowered. "Their idea of exercise is to run around the playground."

"There are plenty of ways to exercise on your own," I said. "I have some books. I even have a video I could lend you."

"We don't have a VCR," she said. "*Or* a TV."

My eyebrows shot up.

"The reception is poor down here," the aunt murmured.

"Couldn't you get an antenna?"

"She thinks TV is the work of the devil," Becca said. "She wants me to read those!" She waved her hand at the shelves of books.

No TV? That could cause any teenager to leave home. I was saved from getting involved in a family argument by a resounding crash. Startled, we all looked toward the kitchen. Juri stuck his head out the door—"Sorry!"—and ducked back again.

I put down my glass and went to see if I could help.

"No, thanks." Juri pushed me quickly out of the kitchen, but not before I caught sight of a box of dried prunes on the counter. I hoped that wasn't dessert.

On my way back to the living room, I glanced in the dining room. Although not illuminated yet, through the shadows I made out a table set for five.

CHAPTER 11

Becca was alone when I returned to the living room.

"Come on, Jo," she said, "Let's take Elsa out to play."

I followed her and the bounding dog outside.

The evening air was cool and fresh, smelling of fallen leaves and the salt marshes nearby. A purple streak on the horizon was all that remained of the day.

"Fetch, Elsa!" Becca threw the ball across the field. We watched the dog roll after it like gray silk.

Drooling and panting, she brought the ball back. "Good girl." Becca wiped her hand on her jeans and threw the ball again. The dog disappeared into the murky twilight.

"Do you have houseguests?" I asked, casually.

"Oh, yeah. This couple came yesterday. My aunt takes in refugees now and then. Helps them get settled. But these two . . ." She made a face.

"What's wrong with them?"

Becca shrugged. "They—"

"Dinner's ready!" The aunt's voice rose from the porch.

She grabbed the ball from Elsa and we went inside.

• • •

Wall sconces cast a mellow glow over the dining room and its furnishings. Art Deco came to mind. The curtains were gray silk. Black-and-white abstract prints donned the walls. The table and chairs were of raw polished wood. Black woven place mats bore chunky white china and silverware with a geometric design. An arrangement of feathery reeds and marsh grasses filled a squat orange vase—the only touch of color in the room. The five place settings, which I had expected to increase to six, had been reduced instead to four. Apparently Becca's houseguests would not be joining us.

Juri served cold salmon, quivering tomato aspic, and steaming rice with almonds. *Why wasn't Becca helping to serve?* Juri also filled the wineglasses, even giving Becca half a glass, in the European tradition.

When Juri was seated, the aunt cut a small piece of salmon, placed it in her mouth, and chewed as if the fish had spines.

Juri brooded over his plate in silence.

Becca ate with the speed and gusto of a normal teenager.

I picked at my food.

"I'm sorry the weather isn't better." The aunt roused herself. "It's beautiful here in the spring."

The autumn weather suited me just fine.

A heavy silence settled over the table. I would have almost welcomed Juri's earlier interrogation. The clink of silver against china increased in volume as the meal wore on. I should have followed my earlier instinct, and left before dinner. My fears about the dried prunes proved groundless; a delicious crème caramel appeared for dessert. But the atmosphere was no warmer. When the last bite had been consumed, I politely excused myself, pleading an urgent errand.

Becca's eyes held a mute plea that I couldn't answer. She followed me out to the car.

"You could have stayed for coffee," she said plaintively.

"If you need me, here's my cell phone number." I scribbled it on a scrap of paper.

She snatched it and ran back to the house.

I was torn between sympathy and irritation. Sympathy—for a kid who shared a house with two self-absorbed adults and no TV. Irritation—at her sassy mouth and lousy manners. She *was* spoiled. I wondered if the aunt was aware of her niece's extracurricular activities. Or was that standard teenage behavior in the new millennium?

Something Sophie's parents would never have to worry about.

Where had that come from? I pounded the steering wheel until my hand was numb.

As I drove down the driveway, I remembered my visit of the night before. The harsh, sexless voice that had called out the window to Juri certainly hadn't belonged to Becca's lethargic aunt. It must have been one of the refugees. Prunes! An image of the bright brown and yellow box rose before me. Not the favorite fruit of most people. Yet, I had seen that box twice in the past few days. There couldn't be too many foreign people in a remote area like Bayfield who fancied prunes. If my hunch was right, it was easy to understand why Becca's houseguests hadn't come down to dinner.

CHAPTER 12

When I walked into the motel, Mr. Nelson was poring over the newspaper.

I greeted him. "I saw our buddies today."

He looked up, puzzled.

"You know. The ones who skipped without paying."

"Oh."

I've seen patients on their way to the OR show more enthusiasm. "But I let them get away."

"Good."

"But they walked off with a night's rent!" I was indignant.

"It's only money." He went back to his newspaper.

It's only money. The words vibrated in my head. It was not a common Manhattan expression.

"Look at this." He shoved the paper under my nose, jabbing his finger at the lead headline.

HUMAN SCARECROW REMAINS A MYSTERY

I bent to read the article.

The body disguised as a scarecrow, discovered in Saul Perkin's field last week, remains unidentified. After . . .

My mind was too full of my own affairs. I couldn't concentrate on the small type. "Mr. Nelson—"

"Paul."

"Paul—could I have a word with you?"

"Sure." Caught by the earnestness of my tone, he laid the paper aside.

"Could you give me the names of those motels that might need my services?"

He looked as if I'd told him he'd won the lottery.

"This is just temporary. A sort of experiment."

He nodded enthusiastically.

"There will be a slight delay," I rattled on. "I've got to get a New Jersey medical license, narcotics licenses, and change my malpractice insurance. And I'll need some time to arrange my affairs in New York—"

"I understand." He was still looking at me as if he was five years old and I'd just handed him a double-decker ice cream cone. All chocolate.

"Then there are the arrangements down here. I'll need a small office, a place to stay, and—"

"No problem." He grinned. "This end will be easy. You can have one of the cabins out front for an office, and any room in the motel is yours."

"That's very kind of you, but I won't be able to pay rent for a month or two—"

"No rent for the office. That cabin's been sitting there, taking up space, since the forties. As for the room—the rent can wait. And if you want to make any changes, you know—paint it, bring in your own furniture—that's fine, too."

"I don't know what to say . . ."

"Not another word. You've made me a very happy man."

And indeed, he seemed changed. Before, he had seemed surrounded by a gray aura, bowed down by some invisible weight. Now he even looked younger. As I turned to go, he stopped me. "By the way, my wife thinks you're great."

"I hardly spoke to her."

"She says you have steady eyes."

My gaze automatically dropped to the floor.

"You'd be surprised how many shifty eyes we get in here."

I thought of the Pillsbury couple. "No, I wouldn't."

"When will you be leaving?"

"Tomorrow, at the crack of dawn." I was glad to escape. Too much adulation made me queasy. Or was it my empty stomach? I had barely touched my gourmet dinner.

At Harry's Bar and Grill (apparently the only food-and-watering place for miles) the bar was horseshoe-shaped, and the stares of the bulls across from me seemed less intent than the night before. Could they be getting used to me? Except for one stare, which was even more intent. Recognition dawned. Robin Hood. I quickly bent to my beer and hamburger.

A few minutes later, I was conscious of someone sliding onto the barstool next to mine. "Does this remind you of Manhattan?" His voice was as cool as shaved ice—useful for conning females.

I turned. "I beg your pardon?" Why did this guy get under my skin? One word from him and I was talking like a New York socialite.

"Name's Tom. I hear you're staying on."

I blinked. Once more the village grapevine had caught me off guard.

"Paul Nelson is a friend of mine," he explained. "I dropped by the motel after you'd left and—"

"Another generation, isn't he?"

He hesitated. "I knew his son."

"He has a son?"

"Had."

Silence. I wanted to know what had happened to the son, but I'd be damned if I'd ask.

"He disappeared."

I looked at him. "As on milk cartons?"

He nodded.

"When?"

He shrugged. "Three years ago."

"Did they try to find him?"

"Oh, sure. Even got the FBI in on it. Nothing turned up. I think the Nelsons have accepted it—finally."

"That he's not coming back."

He nodded.

In a flash, I understood Mr. Nelson's gray aspect—and his expression, *It's only money.*

"What do you think happened?"

"He ran with a wild crowd in high school . . ."

"Yours?"

He ignored this. "He always needed money. Somebody in his crowd had a leather jacket; Nick had to have two leather jackets. His parents—the Nelsons—couldn't keep up with it. They tried. But the Oakview Motor Lodge isn't exactly the Ritz."

"I get the picture." I cut him off. I didn't want a rundown on the Nelsons' financial affairs. "Was he into drugs?"

"His staff of life."

"Is he alive?"

He looked down. "I hope not."

"For his sake or the Nelsons'?"

He raised his eyes to mine and said softly, "I don't care what happened to that bastard."

There didn't seem to be anything more to say. I worked on the remains of my hamburger.

After a minute he said, "Paul's very happy you've decided to stay."

"I know. I only hope I can live up to his expectations." *Where had that crap come from?* "I hafta get back." I dug in my jeans for a tip, snatched up my check, and made a beeline for the cash register.

What's wrong with me? Why antagonize a perfectly nice hunk? Disgusted with myself, I hurried back to the motel in search of sleep—and oblivion. My last thought before I conked out: *I need another man like a hole in the head. Don't I have enough troubles?*

CHAPTER 13

Although I had been away from Manhattan for only forty-eight hours, when I got back to my apartment and checked my phone messages there were half a dozen from my father—the note of panic increasing a few decibels in each one.

"Hi, Dad."

"Thank God. Where've you been?"

"I took a little vacation. Needed to get out of town. Sorry I worried you." (Long ago I'd stopped reminding him that I was twenty-six, twenty-seven, twenty-eight years old and able to take care of myself. When I was a hundred, he'd still worry.)

"Never mind. Where'd you go?"

"Salem, New Jersey."

Dead silence.

"It's near the Delaware Bay. Its main claim to fame is a nuclear power plant."

"What the—?"

"Look, it's a long story—and I just got in. I'll meet you at the diner for dinner." The diner was the Gemini just two blocks from my apartment at Second and Thirty-third. Whenever Dad came into the city, we ate there. Not for us the glitzy, expensive restaurants that catered to the tourist trade. Besides, the food was better.

He grunted his agreement.

• • •

"So that's the plan." I glanced at my father over a pile of shrimp carcasses and one squeezed-to-death lemon segment.

He stared back at me over the naked bones of two pork chops and a parsley sprig that would never rise again.

I was the first to look away. My father's gaze had not been hard to read: *Are you crazy?*

There was some justification for this. The last time I'd seen him, I had described with pride a cocktail party to which all the great names in New York medicine had been invited—and me, too. At the time I'd suspected he'd thought it was silly, but you could never tell with Dad. Maybe it was just my sudden about-face that had thrown him. But more likely, it was the distance it would put between us. Since my mother died (when I was four), I had never lived more than an hour away from him.

"It's just a six-month trial," I murmured. As usual, one of his looks had set off a chain reaction of doubts about my most carefully laid plans.

He tossed his balled-up paper napkin on the table. "When do you leave?"

"In a week."

"Not much time. What about your office? Your apartment?"

"I can rent the office like that!" I snapped my fingers. "And I think I can sublet the apartment."

"You're sure this is—?"

"It's just an experiment, Dad." I cut him off before he could undermine my decision any further. "I can be back in Manhattan tomorrow."

"But your opportunities . . ."

"My credentials are my opportunities."

He sighed. And it was the sigh of someone from another generation—a generation in which education was not as easy to come by, or work as readily available.

He shook his head. Suddenly he looked up. "What about Ken?"

I didn't answer.

"Now I get it."

He didn't, but I let him think he did. He thought I was perfect. Why disillusion him? I had told him about Sophie when it happened, of course. But it was an abbreviated account, omitting such salient points as my misdiagnosis. To spare his feelings, I told myself.

"Shall we go?" I started to pull on my parka.

He couldn't resist one last searching glance for signs of unrequited love. Finding none, he shook his head again and wormed his way into his own parka.

Leaving the glittering amber lights of the diner behind, we headed south on Second Avenue. Usually we linked arms, exchanging heated views on some past or upcoming contest between the Yankees and the Orioles, the Islanders and the Rangers. Tonight we walked in silence with space between us until we hit Thirty-fourth. There we parted, Dad heading across town for his subway while I continued on to Thirty-third.

CHAPTER 14

As I'd told Dad, it was a snap to unload my office. Office space in upscale medical buildings in Manhattan is always at a premium. The apartment was another story. My lease still had six months to go, and my landlord wasn't about to let me worm out of it. I had been planning to call Ken and get him to find me a subletter. He had lived in my apartment for over a year—why shouldn't he take some responsibility? But when I went to dial him, I realized I didn't know where he was. I could call him at work, but he shared an office with a couple of colleagues and I wasn't in the mood for small talk. I could track him down, of course, but this would mean a roundabout phone search through friends, and endless explanations about our split that I didn't feel up to right now. Fortunately, he called me. He had been trying to reach me all weekend. It was an uninspired conversation, but one that ended to my satisfaction—a promise from him to find a subletter for my apartment. Whew! Home free. Now I just had to decide what to store and what to take. Dad had promised to bring his van over to pick up the things I didn't want to take to New Jersey. There was plenty of storage space in the cellar and garage, he assured me. If there was any overflow, there was always the print shop. But I'd have to rent a U-Haul for the remainder.

It took a little over ten days to wind things up. There had been no problem staying on the courtesy staff of my fancy hospital. My colleagues had managed to keep their surprise under wraps. What they said behind my back, I could only guess. I left my savings account untouched in the Manhattan bank (all $200 of it). My final act before leaving the city was to mail the apartment keys to Ken. (He was temporarily sharing a pad on the West Side with a couple of his buddies.) As I walked back down the block from the mailbox toward my overstuffed U-Haul, I felt as giddy as a kid on the first day of summer vacation. Edging the U-Haul out of the parking spot, I pointed it downtown toward the Holland Tunnel.

CHAPTER 15

"You've got a house call!" Paul hailed me as I came in the door to pick up my key.

My mouth did a good imitation of the Grand Canyon.

"It just came." He handed me a slip of paper with a name and number scrawled on it.

"But—" I sputtered, "my Jersey license hasn't—"

He handed me an envelope from the Board of Medical Examiners.

"But my narcotics—"

He handed me two more envelopes from the narcotics bureaus.

The Grand Canyon snapped shut. Apparently New Jersey's bureaucracy was more efficient than New York's. I looked down at the first piece of paper. Amy Nice, Midway Motor Inn, and the phone number. "Midway between what and what?"

"Salem and Bridgeton," he said, and he handed me another slip of paper. This one bore a map that he had drawn himself.

Sheepishly, I thanked him. "Any info on the patient?"

"Seven-year-old girl with hives."

My stomach did a ninety-degree flip. Why couldn't it have been a male octogenarian with a hernia? I considered heading back to the Turnpike. But medical training dies hard. I beat it to the

U-Haul without another word. Hives, if not treated promptly, can spread to the throat and block the air passages.

On the way to the motel I had time to think. I hadn't planned to jump back into practice with an emergency—especially not one involving a child. That nocturnal emergency in the room next to mine had been an unavoidable episode, a chance occurrence not to be repeated. When I decided to come to Bayfield I had planned to ease myself back into practice little by little, starting with a few bad colds, a bee sting, or a case of poison ivy, gradually working my way up to some more serious respiratory infections, an appendectomy maybe, and eventually—say in a year or two—a heart attack. All my patients would be sixty-five or older, people whose lives had been lived to the fullest and, if shortened, would not have too many regrets.

The Midway Motor Inn was a carbon copy of the Oakview Motel, minus the 1930s cabins. But the motel operator bore no resemblance to Paul Nelson. He was a she, with heavy makeup and a hard stare. She directed me to Room 32. I had forgotten how casually I was dressed—in parka, T-shirt, jeans and sneakers—until I saw the startled expression of the neatly groomed woman who opened the door. The only clue she had that I was a doctor was the black medical kit in my left hand.

"Dr. Banks." I offered my right hand. "Excuse the informality of my dress, but I thought I'd better come right away."

"Come in, Doctor."

I stepped into the room and caught the first sight of my patient. Big for seven, the child had taken over the entire double bed and made it her own. The sheets were littered with gum wrappers and comic books. Her eyes were glued to the TV screen. Even from this distance I could see the welts on her stomach. She had pulled up her T-shirt and pulled down her jeans to facilitate easier scratching. Each welt was white and about the size of a quarter.

"Hello, Amy," I said.

She glanced at me briefly.

"After I wash my hands, I'll take a look at that rash."

She began to scratch her stomach vigorously with both hands.

"Try not to do that," I said.

"It itches." She pouted.

I turned to her mother. "May I use your sink?"

"Go right ahead, Doctor." The woman gestured to the bathroom.

When I came back to the bed, Amy had pulled down her T-shirt and pulled up her jeans, hiding her rash from me.

"Let's have a look," I said.

Her lower lip popped out and she shook her head.

I didn't expect much help from the mother. Fragile and feminine-looking, I automatically categorized her as wishy-washy.

"I can't stop the itch unless you let me see what's wrong," I said in my most reasonable tone.

"Let her see!" barked the mother, scaring me more than the child.

Up came the shirt.

So much for my powers of psychoanalysis. Lucky I'd opted for family medicine and not psychiatry. I carefully examined her stomach. "Do you itch anywhere else?"

She shook her head.

I took a tongue blade from my kit and asked her to open her mouth.

She glanced at her mother who was standing behind me. The mouth opened.

"Wider, please."

"It doesn't itch there," she whined, but obeyed.

I pressed her tongue flat with my blade and flashed my light over the back of her throat. Faint white spots were beginning to show on either side. If untreated, they could swell into hives large enough to cut off her breathing. I withdrew the blade.

"Why's your hand shaking?"

Kids notice everything. "I was up all night."

"Why?"

I could feel the mother's eyes lasering into my back.

"My cat was sick," I lied.

"What was wrong with him?"

"Uh—he had a pain." *Get hold of yourself. She's not Sophie.* Sophie was small and delicate with auburn hair, soft gray eyes, and a sweet smile. This kid was big and blond with dark brown eyes and a sullen expression.

"Is he okay now?"

"I think so."

"What's his name?"

"Frankie."

"That's not a good name for a cat."

"It isn't?"

"Nah."

"What's a good cat name?"

"Mustard."

"But my cat's black."

"Licorice, then. You could call him Lick for short."

"That's perfect. He does a lot of licking with that rough tongue of his."

"Why is it rough?"

"To remove loose hair when he's shedding . . ."

We both turned at the interruption.

". . . and other forms of dirt," the mother added.

I glanced around for a wastebasket in which to throw the tongue blade. The mother brought one quickly. I tossed the blade and noted with relief that my hand was steady again. I rummaged in my medical kit. The child watched me carefully. When I drew out a syringe in a see-through wrapper, she squealed and drew back against the headboard.

I laid the syringe on the bedside table. "Amy, I can't tell you this won't hurt. It will—a little."

Her eyes filled and she began to sniffle.

"But I need your help in a little scientific experiment." I picked up the syringe. "I'm going to tell you exactly what this shot will feel like, and afterwards I want you to tell me if I'm right or wrong. You have to concentrate very hard so you can describe how it felt afterwards. Then I can add it to the data I'm collecting for a very important scientific paper. Are you ready?"

She bent her elbow and held her arm tight against her chest.

"Amy!" Her mother's voice was like a pistol shot.

The child stretched out her arm.

As I swabbed her skin with alcohol, I said, "First you're going to feel a pinprick. No more than the prick of a thorn." I tossed the cotton and tore the wrapper off the syringe. "This will be followed by a sting, which will last three seconds." I positioned the needle. "Now, here's the important part." I forced her to look at me. "I want you to count those seconds—one chimpanzee, two chimpanzee, three chimpanzee . . ." I slid the needle in.

With her eyes squeezed shut, she counted, "One chimpanzee, two chimpanzee, three chimpanzee, four chimpanzee." Her eyelids flew open and she looked at me accusingly. "It was *four* seconds."

"Good for you." I smiled, easing the needle out. "You've just made a great contribution to modern science." I took out a pad and pen. At the top I wrote, *Sting lasts 4 seconds.* "Will you sign this, please?" I handed her my ballpoint pen.

She signed.

As I placed a Band-Aid over the puncture, I said, "Thanks to you, the next time I give this shot, I'll have to tell the patient the sting will last four, not three, seconds."

She smiled with satisfaction.

I scrawled a prescription for hydrocortisone cream and handed it to her mother. "This should take care of the itching. And that shot of adrenaline I gave her should prevent the hives from swelling or spreading."

"Thank you, Doctor." She placed the prescription carefully on the bureau. "What do I owe you?"

After a quick calculation, I came up with, "Thirty-five."

She didn't whistle, but looked as if she'd like to.

I thought of explaining that I'd traveled ten miles and the adrenaline had cost ten dollars, but caught myself. No apologies. No excuses. A house call is a house call is a house call. This wasn't the horse-and-buggy days when a loaf of bread cost ten cents, and a cup of coffee, a nickel.

She took a wad of bills from her purse and wordlessly peeled off three tens and a five.

"Are you going to be here long?" I placed the bills in my pocket and wrote out a receipt.

"We'd planned to leave tomorrow."

"If Amy complains of any difficulty breathing or swallowing during the night, be sure to call me—*no matter how late it is.*"

A look of alarm crossed her face.

"It's very unlikely," I reassured her. I turned to Amy. "So long. You have the makings of a great scientist."

She barely nodded, her eyes glued once more to the TV screen.

I climbed into the U-Haul, still packed with my belongings. Before turning the key, I sat a minute, breathing deeply. I had scaled one hurdle. I had treated a child. I turned the key. Now—if only those hives don't swell!

CHAPTER 16

"Come with me to the Craft Fair." Maggie waylaid me as I came in the door.

"Oh, I don't think . . ." I had been up since six, driven the U-Haul from New York, and was still recovering from my first house (motel) call. Even though it was barely noon, I was exhausted. And I still had to unload the U-Haul.

"Come on, Jo. It's a beautiful day, and this is a good way to meet people. . . ."

It *was* a beautiful day. Crisp and cool—a perfect finale to October, before bleak November set in.

"You might pick up a few patients." She gave my arm an extra psychological twist.

"Do they have food?" My stomach was in its usual cavernous state.

"Are you kidding?" Her eyes brightened. "There's the Baptist bake sale, Betsy Hawkin's homemade ice cream, Charlie Meek's old-fashioned waffles . . ."

"I'm coming, I'm coming." I followed her out to the parking lot.

The Craft Fair was a surprise. Instead of a few ramshackle booths manned by a couple of local yokels, there was an extensive network of vendors from all over the eastern seaboard. Basket weavers from Connecticut, cabinetmakers from Maine, a silversmith from the Smokies, a quilter from Lancaster. The grassy aisles between the booths were packed with people from as far away as Philadelphia, New York, and Baltimore. How did I know? Their cars were parked nose to tail along both sides of the main street, and I read their license plates.

"I thought Bayfield was a secret," I whined to Maggie. "How come half the East Coast is here?"

"Advertising." She slapped a brochure into my hand.

On the front was a picture of a spinning wheel, and on the back, a detailed map showing how to get here from north, south, east, and west.

"Come on, Jo. You're dragging. We don't want to miss the auction."

"Auction? I've never been to an auction," I wailed. "What do I do?"

"Just sit on your hands and keep your mouth shut," Maggie advised. She had spied two empty seats and was burrowing past a row of bulky knees to claim them.

"Aren't we lucky?" She settled into one seat and pulled me down into the other.

The auction was already in progress. The auctioneer was taking bids on a hideous purple vase.

"Eight dollars. Do I hear nine? Nine dollars. Do I hear ten?"

I didn't feel it necessary to sit on my hands for this one. I wasn't even tempted. I scanned the audience. Mostly middle-aged white. Come to think of it, African, Asian, and Hispanic faces were a rarity here. The most common people of color were *red*necks. I felt a pang of homesickness.

"Now, ladies and gentlemen, we have here an oil painting that rivals the *Mona Lisa*. The frame alone is worth a hundred. Look at that gilding."

He stressed the frame because the picture was not likely to attract this audience. Scarlet-coated huntsmen jumping a fence were not about to appeal to the honest yeoman farmers of Bayfield. The painting *with* frame went for $25.

I yawned and glanced over at Maggie. To my surprise she was sitting forward, her eyes fixed on the auctioneer. The auction catalog lay open on her lap with a number of items circled in red.

"Now, folks . . ." Having disposed of the elegant painting, he could afford to be more informal. ". . . we have here a special prize." He turned his back for a moment to receive the next item from one of his helpers. Awkward and bulky, they dragged it to the front of the platform and began tearing off its wrappings. "What have we here?" the auctioneer asked, as if ignorant of the contents. As the last wrappings fell to the ground, there was a general intake of breath. With floppy hat, painted smile, arms and legs akimbo, it was an exact replica of that endearing figure from *The Wizard of Oz*—the Scarecrow.

"What am I bid for this fine fellow?"

The audience laughed.

"Look how strong he is." The auctioneer slapped his chest. "Do I hear fifty dollars?"

The audience roared.

"Oh, come now. This is no ordinary fellow." He snapped the strap of his denim overall.

More laughter, but no bids.

"Spring's around the corner, folks." He adopted a more serious tone. "And with spring come the crows!"

Silence.

"Crows that'll gobble up your freshly sowed seeds!"

"Five." A farmer in the front row raised his hand.

"I have five dollars. An insult to this handsome fellow. Do I hear ten?"

"Ten."

"I have ten. Do I hear twenty?"

"Twenty." Maggie nearly jumped out of her seat when I spoke up.

"Twenty-five?" asked the auctioneer.

Silence.

"Going . . . going . . . gone." *Bang* went the mallet. "To the lady in the third row."

Everyone turned to see who would be crazy enough to pay twenty dollars for a scarecrow.

Maggie ducked her head, embarrassed to be sitting next to me. "What did you do that for?" she whispered fiercely.

I shrugged and stared straight ahead. How could I explain to this practical, down-to-earth woman that *The Wizard of Oz* was my favorite book in the whole world, and the Scarecrow my favorite fictional character of all time? My dad had read it to me every night until I was able to read. Then I had read it until the book was as tattered and torn as—well, a scarecrow.

The auctioneer had gone on to something else, a set of silver spoons that Maggie was interested in. She bid seventy-five dollars, but lost them to a dealer for eighty. Seventy-five was her limit, she whispered. And when she set limits, she stuck to them. Old-fashioned, our Maggie. Later she landed a set of pink English china she'd had her heart set on, for fifty dollars. She was thrilled. "Now I'll have something decent to serve Thanksgiving dinner on." She glowed. "Let's go."

I followed her out of the row and down to an area behind the auctioneer's platform, where we paid cash for our purchases to a tired-looking woman behind a rickety card table. She checked off our items on a long list and stamped them PAID with a rubber stamp.

Because the cartons of dishes were heavy, Maggie borrowed a handcart and pushed them across the bumpy field. I trailed behind, lugging my scarecrow. Some people snickered as we passed, but I didn't care. He was a fine fellow and just what I needed to fill that bare corner in my bed/sitting room. If he got lonely, I'd play my Black Crows CD for him. Yuk, yuk.

About halfway to the car, Maggie stopped short, her eyes riveted to the back of a young man, chunky and dark, in jeans and a black leather jacket, who was crossing the field a few yards ahead of us. Maggie dropped the cart and took off after him. Luckily, I was right behind her; I caught the cart and saved the dishes. At the sound of her footsteps, the young man turned quickly. Maggie fell back, as if he had struck her. There was an awkward pause before the man turned and walked on. Maggie stumbled back to me.

Shocked by her pallor, I was afraid she was going to faint. I took her arm. "What was that all about?"

She took a deep breath. "He looked like Nick."

I put my arm around her and held her close. After a moment, she drew away and we continued on to the car.

Carefully, I laid the scarecrow on the backseat and went to help Maggie load her dishes into the trunk. As we left, I noticed she didn't bother locking the car. Having grown up in New York, this was one Bayfield habit I would never get used to.

"I'll take the cart back," I offered.

"Thanks. I'll meet you at the Baptist bake sale booth in fifteen minutes." Her color had returned and, deciding she might want a few minutes to herself, I let her go. As I trundled the cart at a more leisurely pace, I thought about Nick. He had been missing for three years, Tom said. Poor Maggie. She would never give up hope, I was afraid, until she saw his body lowered into the ground.

Two rednecks passed me, heading in the opposite direction. They didn't even glance my way. Strange. That type usually stared at anything female, if only to make her feel uncomfortable.

After I returned the cart I pushed my way through the crowd of country folk, suburbanites, kids, and dogs. There were even a few sheep wandering around loose, left over from the wool-shearing demonstration. I moseyed along, pausing to examine a finely crafted rocking chair, an intricately woven shawl, and a handmade salad bowl. In an open space, a man was demonstrating a bow and arrow. His back to me, he drew the string taut and let go. *Zing!* The arrow zipped through the air and landed very near the bull's-eye a hundred feet away.

"Nice," I spoke involuntarily.

The archer turned.

"Robin Hood!" I blurted.

"Dorothy!" he retorted.

I felt my face flush. He'd forgotten my name! And what was worse, he had mistaken me for someone else.

"What are you going to bid on next? A lion or a tin woodsman?" He smiled, laying his bow aside.

Finally getting the joke, I said, "How did you know . . . ?"

"Everybody's talking about it. How the doctor's going to practice her appendectomies on a scarecrow."

I had to laugh. "I see you're giving the deer a rest today."

"Yes. I was asked to show off my great skills, and as you can see, the audience is overwhelming."

"What's all this?" I wandered into his booth and stood looking at some tools spread out on a workbench.

"That's where I make my bows and arrows."

"You make your own?"

He nodded. "Like the Lenapes."

"Lenapes?"

"The Lenni Lenapes—the Indians who settled in these parts."

"Native Americans."

"Pardon."

"Never mind." Trying to convert Bayfielders to political correctness was a lost cause. "Show me how you do it."

He glanced at me, not sure he had heard right. Convinced I was in earnest, he picked up a stone from the workbench and handed it to me. It was about four by five inches, hard and black.

"That's obsidian. When freshly flaked it can be four hundred times sharper than surgical steel." He sat down on a wooden stool and pulled a thick leather pad across his knees. Placing the stone on the pad, he studied it as a sculptor might. Then he took a small mallet from the workbench and tapped the stone. A piece of the stone fell away. He tapped the stone at another spot. Another piece fell away. The stone began to take on a sharp, triangular shape.

I watched, fascinated in spite of myself. "How did you do that?"

"You study the grain of the stone and locate its flaws before you tap it. Then the pieces will usually fall away where you want them to. Its called knapping."

"As in kid?"

"No. K-n-a-p . . . and the people who do it are called knappers."

"And that's the way the Indians made their arrowheads?"

"It's one way."

"And you make your bows, too?"

He handed me the one he had just used. A beautiful instrument. Smooth, flexible, honey-colored. I gave it back. He demonstrated how it would bend without breaking.

"Can I try?" a tow-headed boy spoke up. He had been watching from a distance.

"Sure." Tom gave it to him. The bow was about two feet taller than the boy. "Here." He led him nearer to the target and set his hands in the right positions on the bow. "Now look straight at the bull's-eye . . ."

He had a nice way with the kid. Suddenly, I remembered Maggie. "Gotta go," I said.

I smelled the Baptist bake table before I saw it, and began to salivate. Maggie was scanning the crowd for me. "I thought you'd gone home," she said.

"Sorry, I got involved with the archer."

"Oh, Tom Canby. We call him the Bowman around here. Now what will you have, Jo?" She indicated the array of succulent baked goods spread out on the table. "Chocolate cake, cherry pie, lemon squares . . . ?"

"Lemon squares," I said quickly. There was a bakery in Queens that had sold them. I used to pick them up after school when I was flush with a new allowance.

Maggie turned to one of the Baptists behind the table. "A dozen lemon squares, please. Take one, Jo, before she wraps them up," she urged.

She didn't have to urge me twice. It was sublime. Just the right consistency. A perfect blend of sweet and tart, the pastry melted on my tongue.

After two more stops, for a heaping dish of strawberry ice cream and a waffle the size of a large frying pan, I was ready to go home. Maggie agreed and we made our way across the field for the fourth time that day. Before I got into the car, I glanced in the backseat. It was empty.

"But who would want to steal a scarecrow?" I moaned.

"Some kid probably. A prank."

"Some prank. I'd like to get my hands on . . ."

"Now, now," Maggie soothed, pulling into the motel parking lot.

"If only you'd locked your car," I blurted.

Maggie looked shocked. "But we never lock . . ."

"I know. I know. Because Bayfield is so safe." I climbed out. "Well, it isn't safe." I slammed the door. "And I'm out twenty bucks."

"That's enough," Maggie said.

I looked at her and shut up. What was the loss of a scarecrow compared to the loss of a son?

"Well, well," Mr. Nelson greeted us. "Did you spend all our retirement money?"

Maggie told him about the scarecrow.

He was genuinely upset. "I can probably find you another one," he said slowly. "Or we can make one."

"Make one?"

"Sure. Nothing to it. All you need are some strong poles, some old clothes, plenty of straw and twine."

"When?"

"How about Sunday morning—around church time?"

Maggie frowned and left abruptly. (I wouldn't find out why until much later.)

"It's a date," I said. "And I'll provide the clothes."

I took off for my room, feeling much better. I didn't know what I loved Paul for more—offering to make a scarecrow, or *not* asking me why I'd bid on one.

CHAPTER 17

When the U-Haul was emptied, I realized it was time to return it. I'd spotted a U-Haul lot on the main road. But once returned, I would have no wheels. No wheels meant—no house calls. This revelation came to me with a shock as I sat slumped in the front seat of the U-haul, recovering from single-handedly wrestling my furniture up the narrow, iron staircase to the second floor, down the long corridor, and into my room. Paul had suggested that I wait until evening when Jack-the-night-clerk could help me. But, not one to put things off, I went ahead and did it myself. The only real problem was the easy chair. There was nothing easy about it. It weighed a ton and its ungainly shape refused to bend around corners. The stereo was no lightweight, either. However, the move was done. Now I had to face this new problem. The obvious solution was to rent a car until I could buy a secondhand one, but that would be an expensive proposition. Slowly my eyes focused on something through the smudged windshield—something I had passed many times on my way in and out of the motel office, but had never really registered. Propped against the wall by the door, a hand-lettered FOR SALE sign dangled from its handlebars.

"Paul."

He looked up from his crossword puzzle.

"How much for that bike outside?"

"Bike?"

"Motorcycle. The one for sale."

He shook his head. "Not for sale." And went back to his puzzle.

"What do you mean? There's a sign on it."

He nodded without looking up. "I forgot to take it off."

He was a lousy liar.

"Does it run?"

He shrugged.

Maybe he thought I couldn't afford it. "Look, I might have to pay you in installments, but you'd get your money."

Maggie appeared from somewhere in the back to take over desk duty from her husband. "Did someone mention money?" Her sharp eyes grew sharper.

"I want to buy that bike outside. The one with the FOR SALE sign on it. But your husband says it's not for sale."

She looked reflectively at the smooth top of her husband's head—still bent over the crossword puzzle. "Come back in an hour," she said quietly.

Her husband's face reared up wearing a belligerent expression. I exited quickly.

As I headed for my room, I was hurt. I thought Mr. Nelson—Paul—liked me. Why not sell me his bike? *His* bike? A picture of the elderly gentleman sprinting down the highway flashed through my mind. *Jackass.* His son's bike. *Shit.* I entered my room and kicked the door shut. But I felt better. Paul did like me. He just liked his son more.

I filled the next hour rearranging my room. When I had walked in, it had resembled a used furniture store. But after some judicious jostling and juggling, it gradually took on a more homey atmosphere. I replaced the two ugly vinyl chairs with the easy chair; the bulbous terracotta lamp with a sleek metal one; the orange bedspread and acid green blanket with my plum-colored down comforter; and the greasy clipper ship plowing through an oily sea with crisp Dufy sailboats dancing on a sparkling Mediterranean.

The acre of bureau easily accommodated my stereo and VCR

at one end and my microwave and coffee maker at the other. And there was still plenty of room in between for my toilet articles, i.e., two lipsticks (one summer, one winter), a comb, and a bottle of eau de cologne for those extra special occasions. My computer and printer ended up on the desk in the corner. I stuck a Miles Davis CD in the stereo and stretched out on the comforter. As soon as I could afford it, I'd chuck this king-size monster and buy myself a futon that would convert into a couch during the day. And cover the carpet with some colorful throw rugs. Then all evidence of motel decor would be destroyed. As the mellow strains of jazz filled my ears, I surveyed my new home with satisfaction. I was about to doze off when I wearily checked my watch. The hour had flown. I jumped up and narrowly missed breaking my neck on the discarded furniture I had left in the hallway. Making a mental note to call Maintenance (i.e., Jack-the-night-clerk) to cart them away, I sprinted down the stairs to the office.

I don't know what arm-twisting technique Maggie used on her husband but when I came in she said brightly, "Four-fifty. Fifty down, the rest when you have it."

"That's not enough," I blurted. It was a '97 Honda. "Eight hundred minimum." What was I doing—haggling up? But then, everything in South Jersey was upside down.

"Final offer." Maggie's mouth was a firm line.

There was just so much upward haggling a New Yorker was capable of. "It's a deal." I shrugged.

"Why don't you try it out?" She drew a key from the desk drawer.

"Thanks." I reached for it.

"You *have* ridden before?" She held on to the key.

"Oh, sure. My dad had one when I was growing up. I've been riding since I was four."

Her eyebrows shot up.

"I mean—with my dad. But I've ridden by myself off and on since I was sixteen."

Her eyebrows slipped back into place and she relinquished the key.

I headed for the door.

"Wait!" She held up a white helmet.

I came back and tried it on. A loose fit, but nothing that some cotton batting or a little newspaper wouldn't remedy.

"Don't ever ride without it!" She was back in Mary Poppins mode.

"No, ma'am!"

CHAPTER 18

I pulled off the FOR SALE sign and tossed it in the Dumpster. The seat was a better fit than the helmet and—wonder of wonders—the motor started right up. With a flurry of exhaust and a few backfires I zoomed out of the parking lot onto Route 551. As usual, traffic was light. The only other vehicle was a beatup Chevy pickup doing about forty. I passed it easily and headed for the bay. One trip to Mike's and this baby would be ready for anything. A real crotch rocket!

The temperature had dropped. The wind made my face tingle and my eyes water. Goggles, gloves, and biking boots would head my next list of acquisitions.

The bay was dark. A pale streak of lavender stained the horizon. When I shut off the bike, the motor still throbbed in my ears. I dismounted and walked to the water's edge. The mud had frozen and the hard bumps and ruts bored through the soles of my sneakers. As I stood looking toward Delaware, there was a rustle in the reeds to my left. A great blue bird with a neck like a shepherd's crook rose. Its wings spanned a couple of yards. Without effort, it glided—talons skimming the water—and settled onto a piece of driftwood about a hundred feet away. Drawing its wings closely into its sides, it became as still as the wood it was resting on.

For some reason, the Chrysler building came to mind. This was the time of night that its lights came on. It was my favorite building and I often paused to look up at it—like the greenest tourist. Nature wasn't everything. Humans had done a few things, too.

The lavender streak was gone. The first stars had broken out. I straddled my bike and, keeping the motor low, trundled home at thirty miles per hour. Home? Since when had a two-star motel become "home"?

Since now.

Back in my motel room, I began to fret over the hives case I'd seen that morning. My beeper had been silent all afternoon. I checked to make sure it was turned on. It was. Should I call her mother? No way. Unprofessional. She had *my* number. I was available. That's all that was required. What I needed were more patients; then I wouldn't worry about just one. I reached for the TV remote and tried to concentrate on a sitcom. Eventually I dozed off, but it was a fitful sleep. I kept dreaming about hives the size of ostrich eggs. Slowly the night passed with no outburst from my beeper. At 7:00 A.M. I called the Midway Motor Inn. "Mrs. Nice, please."

"Sorry, she and her little girl just checked out."

"Thanks." I fell into a deep and dreamless sleep.

CHAPTER 19

Church bells woke me.

Sunday.

I jumped out of bed. There was so much to do.

Abruptly, I realized my options were limited. In this neck of the woods people probably still observed Sundays religiously, getting all gussied up and piling into churches and meeting houses, then returning home to gorge themselves on huge roast beef or chicken dinners (without a single thought for calories or cholesterol) and dozing the rest of the afternoon away.

Indignation—or jealousy?

Well, at least I could take a ride on my new bike. I had returned the U-Haul the night before. Paul had kindly followed me to the local center and given me a ride back in his pickup.

I drove the bike slowly, taking in the soft autumnal colors—lemon, rust, and rose. Autumn was different here from New England. Instead of blasting you out of your seat, it sort of eased its way into your bloodstream—lowering your blood pressure.

A field of empty cornstalks to my right, a woods to my left, and I knew the Sheffield farm would be coming up around the next bend. Maybe Becca would like to see my bike (if she wasn't in Sunday school). As I bumped up the driveway, I spied her on the porch. She was sitting on the swing, her bright head bent over something in her lap. She was so absorbed, she didn't hear me.

"Want a ride?"

She looked up. Tossing her sketchbook aside, she was off the porch in two bounds. "When did you get it?"

"Yesterday." I handed her my helmet. "Put it on and hop on the back."

When she was settled, I said, "Now, put your arms around my waist and hold on tight."

I felt her thin arms pressing against my ribs.

"Okay?"

"Uh-huh," she mumbled into my back.

A swath of birds, like black cloth, rose from a field on our left and settled in a field on our right.

The empty windows of an abandoned barn framed the empty sky beyond.

It was the sky here that really got me. Instead of snatching glimpses of it between tall buildings, it spread out all around you, wrapping you up in it.

I pulled off the road and stopped. Becca slid off and rolled in the brown grass like a puppy.

"Well?" I said.

"Fabulous. Is that how you're going to make your house calls?"

"Yep."

"Cool."

I dismounted and sat on the grass beside her. "So what are you going to be when you grow up?" I bit my tongue. I'd always hated people who asked me that when I was thirteen.

"Rich."

"You're kidding?"

"Nope." She yawned.

I remembered how she had ordered Juri around. Her aunt was really irresponsible, not demanding more of her. "You'd be surprised how boring rich can be."

"How would you know?"

Fresh. "I've seen it in the movies," I said.

"That's fiction. In real life rich people are happy. The poor are a drag."

I was about to ask, *How many poor do you know?* but held my tongue. Instead I asked, "How come Juri does all the work at your house?"

"Juri?" She said his name as if she had to think who he was.

"Yes. Is he sort of a house man, or . . . ?"

"Handyman. He's a relative who lives off us. That's how he pays for his keep, a kind of—dogsbody." She seemed delighted at having found just the right word.

My dad would have smacked her. "I see. Your aunt's brother?"

"No. A cousin. Her brothers were all killed in the uprising."

"Uprising?"

"The Prague Spring," she said casually. "My aunt's Czech." She rolled away from me, as if the conversation bored her.

I had only the dimmest recollection of the Prague Spring. One of those endless failed uprisings against the Communists in Central Europe. I'd probably skimmed over it in some history survey course, while concentrating on the really important stuff— biology and organic chemistry. "Dubcek!" The name sprang out of my subconscious. "Wasn't he the hero of the Prague Spring?"

She nodded.

"Where is he now?"

"He died."

"Oh."

"In a car accident."

Becca was sitting up now, chewing on a stalk of dry grass. Her hair was a russet halo in the noon sun.

"Have you ever been to Czechoslovakia?" I asked.

"The Czech Republic," she corrected. "I was born in Prague, but when my parents died my grandfather sent me over here to live with my aunt."

"How old were you?"

"Four."

"Do you want to go back?"

She shook her head vehemently.

I was surprised. I'd heard that Prague was one of the most beautiful cities in the world. And now that it was free . . . "Not even to visit?"

For answer, she hopped onto my bike seat and felt for the ignition key. Fortunately I'd had the foresight to remove it. "When you're sixteen, you can try it," I said.

"Sixteen?" she repeated, as if she would never live to such a ripe old age. But she got off the seat and arranged herself on the back as before.

When I dropped her off at her house, I accompanied her onto the porch. I wanted to take a look at that sketchbook. It lay where she had left it, facedown on the swing. When I sat down, the swing creaked. I turned the book over.

The page was filled with sketches of the barn across the driveway. Becca had drawn parts of the building from different angles. They were surprisingly accurate.

"Hey, these are good." I half expected her to snatch the book away from me. Instead, she slid down beside me and examined the sketches critically. "Do you really think so?"

I nodded. "Your perspective is right on target. And you have a good eye for detail." I pointed to her rendering of some hardware on the barn door.

Flipping through the rest of the book, I found it full of equally good drawings of local farmhouses, outbuildings, and more barns. On the last page was a sketch of the cooling tower of the nuclear power plant, casting its bulky shadow across a field. What surprised me was the sameness of the subject matter. No people, no animals, no trees. "You only draw buildings?"

"That's what I like." She grabbed the book and shut it in a single motion.

"But there aren't many around here," I said, "and they're all pretty much the same."

"That's why I wanted to go to New York."

I looked at her. "You mean that's why you were hitching that day?"

She nodded.

So she hadn't been running away. She'd been running toward. "I'll take you to New York," I said.

Her sullen expression vanished. Her face lit up from inside—like a jack-o'-lantern. "You will?"

"Sure."

"When?"

"At Christmas," I promised impulsively, unaware that this was one promise I would not be able to keep.

I stood up. Becca didn't move, but sat silently smiling into space.

"Time for breakfast." Her aunt came out on the porch. When she saw me she smiled and said, "Won't you join us?" She was wearing a colorful silk kimono, sandals, and her makeup looked as if it had taken hours to apply. She wasn't smoking, but looked as if she should be—an exotic, foreign brand in an elegant ivory holder.

"I shouldn't . . ."

"Jo . . ." Becca came out of her trance to plead.

I looked from one to the other. It would be a way to check on those houseguests. "Okay." I nodded.

Again the table was set with a linen cloth, linen napkins, real silverware, and china. But with only two places this time. The aunt hastily added a third place for me. This time Juri was nowhere in sight and the food was not gourmet quality. Cereal, orange juice, coffee, and bagels made up the simple fare. As the aunt served the food, it was hard not to stare at her hands. Pale, tapered fingers with meticulously manicured nails that moved with a sure grace. Only the right-hand index finger was marred at the knuckle—by a black smudge. As before, she made polite conversation. "How do you like Bayfield by now?"

"I love it," I said, surprising myself. "It has a serenity you don't find in New York. I never tire of the sky. In Manhattan you can only see bits and pieces, but here it spreads out all around you, and . . . good grief, I didn't mean to go all poetic." I blushed.

"Not at all. I feel the same way." The aunt sipped her coffee, seeming in no hurry to eat.

I doubted that she spent much time looking at the sky. She didn't seem the outdoor type. How had such a hothouse plant ended up with a farmer in South Jersey? There had to be a story here. "Becca is a very talented artist," I said.

"Do you feel that, too?"

Becca squirmed.

"She just showed me some of her sketches. Have you ever thought of giving her art lessons?"

"You mean send her to art school?"

"Well, no. I meant now. I imagine her talent is far beyond her eighth-grade art teacher. There must be some bona fide artists in South Jersey who would be willing to give her lessons."

Becca was listening intently.

"I hadn't thought of that. After school, you mean? Or on Saturdays?"

I nodded eagerly. Not only would it help Becca's artistic talent, it would keep her occupied and off the motel circuit.

"Hmm. Would you like that, Becca?"

"Yes." The one word, spoken emphatically, conveyed the enthusiasm of a thousand.

"I'll look into it." She finally broke off a piece of bagel and began to nibble.

The conversation turned to other topics, but I felt the aunt was sincere in her concern for her niece and would follow up my suggestion. She lived in another world, and every now and then she needed somebody to push her into this one.

· · ·

When I left, Becca came out with me. Not being one to beat around the bush, I asked, "Where are your houseguests?"

"Around."

Since no more information was forthcoming, I switched to another topic. "How did your aunt meet your uncle?"

"She and my mother came on a tour to the States when they were girls—way before I was born. My aunt met my uncle at a country fair." Becca straddled my bike, gripped the handlebars, and made obnoxious motor noises. "Brrr, brrr."

"What were your mother and aunt doing in the boondocks?"

"Their tour guide thought they should see an American farm as part of their education." She imitated a haughty tour guide.

I had a fleeting vision of the two elegant Czech women tiptoeing among the cow turds.

"Uncle Richard was demonstrating his milking machine at the fair—we still had cows then—and it was love at first sight. Brrr, brrr."

"Your aunt *is* beautiful," I said.

"Is she?" Becca looked up, honestly amazed.

"Oh, yes."

She shrugged. "So, my mother went back to Prague by herself and my aunt stayed here and married my uncle."

"What does your aunt do with herself here, day after day?"

"Oh, she writes poetry and sends it to little magazines." Becca wrinkled her nose.

That explained the black smudge. A true romantic, she probably used India ink and a quill.

"Has she published?" God, I was nosy. My excuse? I was looking after Becca's welfare.

"Once. When the Communists left Czechoslovakia, she wrote a poem and it was published in the Prague newspaper."

I made a mental note to ask to see it sometime.

Becca made a ninety-degree turn on the bike seat and gazed backward over the field.

"Was your mother beautiful, too?"

She reached into her jean's pocket and pulled out a worn black-and-white snapshot. Despite the spidery cracks, I could see she was even more beautiful than her sister. "Was her hair red like yours?"

Becca nodded. Grabbing the photo, she took off running across the field. Either she had decided to chase a butterfly, or . . . the conversation had become too personal.

As I drove away, Juri emerged from the barn. I waved. He didn't wave back. Maybe he didn't recognize me on my new wheels.

CHAPTER 20

When I walked in, helmet in hand, Paul beckoned me over to the desk. "I've got all the stuff in the basement," he whispered. "Have you got the clothes?"

"I'll get them," I whispered back, falling easily into The Great Scarecrow Conspiracy.

My closet yielded a ragged pair of jeans, some old hiking boots, and a tattered Columbia sweatshirt. The sweatshirt gave me pause. We had been through a lot together. Football games, classes, frat parties, and exams. Even—in bed together, on cold nights. *But you're not giving it up,* I assured myself. *You're just lending it to a friend.* I grabbed it and the other clothes and hurried downstairs.

The motel basement was a disappointment. The cinderblock walls were a dull gray, and the slit-like windows let in only a wan light, casting pale, formless shadows on the concrete floor. What had I expected—my great-grandmother's attic, complete with old trunks spilling over with fringed shawls, patchwork quilts, and lace petticoats? The only objects stored here were a couple of exhausted mattresses and a rolled-up remnant of the shit-brown carpet that covered the floors of all the rooms and corridors upstairs.

"Over here!"

Peering through the gloom, I spotted Paul at the far end.

Under a single lightbulb, he was bending over a table—a piece of plywood set on two carpenter's horses.

I laid my bundle of clothes on the table.

"Great. Now we're all set." He had already constructed a solid T by nailing two sturdy poles together. It leaned against the wall. Beside it stood a bail of hay and an enormous ball of twine. What intrigued me most was the pair of huge red long johns, complete with flap, spread out on the table.

"My contribution," he said, following my glance. "They hold the straw better than anything."

As I watched, he began pulling handfuls of straw from the bail and stuffing it into the legs of the long-johns. When he had filled one leg to bursting, he tied it off neatly at the ankle, cut the twine with a pair of shears, and began filling the other one.

"It'll settle once we hang him," he answered my unasked question.

"Can't I do something?"

"Sure." He tossed me a thermal shirt with long sleeves, size XXX. "Start filling that."

When I had finished, we connected our two parts with gigantic safety pins and added my jeans and sweatshirt. The result was a fantastic, headless monster—half Frankenstein creation, half Columbia linebacker. I christened him Ichabod after Washington Irving's headless horseman. (I *had* studied a few things besides biology and organic chemistry.)

"That where you went to school?" Paul tapped the black letters spread across Ichabod's new chest.

I nodded. "But football was never our strong point."

"We wanted our boy to go to college," he said. "Rutgers. But he was always more interested in tinkering with his bike than reading books. He ended up at the local vocational school, in the plumbing class."

"That's a good trade. Very lucrative," I said. "My dad did both. He's a printer. He went to college and then opened his own print shop. He's had a lifetime of tinkering, and I don't know any man who's been happier—with his career, at least."

"Huh."

"I took a boyfriend of mine to his print shop once. And you know what he said? 'Your father's such an intelligent man, why doesn't he open a chain of print shops and just manage them?' He missed the whole point. Jackass!"

Paul stopped fussing with the scarecrow and looked at me. "I think I'd like your father."

Together, we held our headless monster up to the wooden T to see if he was a good fit. Perfect. We took him down again.

"How did you come to be a doctor?"

"My dad's idea. I liked to tinker, too. I would have been happy hanging around the print shop. But Dad had other plans. He had this idea that his only child should have a "profession," not just a trade like him. He didn't know that medicine was going to turn into a corporate monster. . . ." I fit a sneaker to one straw leg, twisted its laces around the ankle, and pulled them tight. ". . . And instead of having an office on the corner—their own private domain—they'd be assigned a cubical, á la *Dilbert*, with *Ivan* watching them—in the form of government agencies, insurance companies, peer-review committees . . ."

Paul looked at me quizzically.

"Sorry. I'll get off my soapbox." I looked at our new creation critically. "What about the head?"

From a paper bag, Paul pulled out a deflated basketball. With a bicycle pump, he pumped the ball until it was about the size of an average human head and sealed it off. Before I could beef about the tangerine color and the lack of features, he whipped out a beige tote bag and pulled it over the ball.

"And how . . . ?"

Before I could finish, Paul produced from his pocket a spool of heavy thread and a wicked-looking needle. "I used to mend sails," he said, and went to work sewing the bottom of the tote bag to the top of my Columbia sweatshirt. When he had finished, our monster had a head, but no neck. Oh, well, most linebackers were neckless, too.

"He needs a hat." Sadly, I thought of my stolen scarecrow's floppy straw hat.

From his magical paper bag, Paul drew a straw hat, almost identical to that of the other scarecrow.

"I'll leave the face up to you," he said, pressing a box of magic markers into my hand. "You're the one who's going to have to live with him."

The box was marked *waterproof*.

"That's in case you ever own a field and want to put him in it."

He had thought of everything.

I set to work to make a face as close to the one of my friend in *The Wizard of Oz* as possible. Two bright blue eyes, a pink nose, and a scarlet, upturned mouth.

"He looks more like a clown," Paul observed.

I shrugged. I never claimed to be an artist.

"He looks cheerful, at least. Come on. It's time to hang him up," he said.

Together, with the rest of the twine, we anchored him to the cross.

"This feels sort of like a crucifixion," I murmured.

Paul, intent on his work, made no reply.

When we were done, we stepped back to admire our masterpiece.

"Not bad," Paul said. "If I do say so myself."

"It's a shame he should be denied his life's work," I said. "He ought to have a crack at scaring crows."

"Well, you could lend him out in the spring. I know a farmer who would be glad to get him. Old man Perkins. He lost one recently."

"Stolen?" I asked glumly.

He nodded. "And someone put a dead man in its place."

"Oh, yeah." I remembered the news article.

"They still haven't identified the body."

"How come?"

"Under the scarecrow outfit, he was stark naked."

"Couldn't they trace him through his dental work or DNA?"

"They tried all that, but it seems he was from out of town. A stranger."

"What's going on down there?" Maggie was back from church.

"Coming!" Paul shouldered our new creation.

As he started up the stairs, Ichabod's hat fell off. Despite his fine new head, I'm afraid that name would stick. (Just so long as no one called him "Icky.") I grabbed the hat and followed them up the stairs.

"There's my hat!" cried Maggie. "I was looking all over for it."

"Whoops!" I handed it to her.

Paul ignored my glare.

CHAPTER 21

After introducing Ichabod to his new quarters, I took off on my bike again. I was able to say "my" now with more authority. I had just presented Maggie with a check for that first installment.

I decided to tool around the neighborhood. I wanted to familiarize myself with the territory, so when (if) I had another house call, I would know how to get there.

When I had mastered the five square miles around the Oakview Motor Lodge, I decided to go further afield. ("Afield" is right. That's all there was.) I had brought a map, but of course there were no road signs, which rendered it practically useless. A compass would have been more to the *point*. I snickered at my own joke. (There was no one for miles to share it with.)

Pausing at a remote intersection (they were all remote), I noticed a bright green field in the midst of all the brown ones. Green in November? Puzzling over this freak of nature, I heard a pickup truck trundle up behind me. I didn't move. There was plenty of room for it to go around me.

The motor behind me continued to throb and a faintly familiar male voice shouted, "Lost?"

Turning, I saw Robin Hood. For once his expression was uncool. Dumbstruck was the only word for it. Immediately spoiling my advantage, I grinned.

Matching my grin, he climbed out and came over.

(The desolate nature of South Jersey can be proved by the fact that not a single vehicle passed us during our exchange.)

"Did I wake you?" He had recovered his cool.

"I was just wondering why that field is so bright green in the middle of November."

"Winter wheat," he said.

"Since you're so smart, what kind of bird lives there?" I pointed to an elaborate black and yellow cone fitted to the top of a tall, stainless steel pole.

"A noisy one." He laughed. "That's an emergency siren for the nuclear power plant. There are dozens of them around here."

That shut me up.

"Where you headed?" He reached for my map.

"I'd like to get back to the Oakview Motor Lodge."

"That's easy. You're here." He pointed to a crossroad. "Crab's Neck and Possum Hollow roads."

How I longed for Fifth Avenue and Forty-second Street! "They have a peculiar habit of not supplying road signs around here." I was instantly horrified at my snide Madison Avenue tone.

"Oh, they supply them all right. But as soon as the signs go up, they take 'em down."

"They? Who? Kids?"

He shook his head. "Grownups, I'm afraid."

"Why?"

"They don't want people to find this place. The wrong people."

"Like me?"

He shrugged.

"Don't they ever get caught?"

"They're good at it. Besides, there's sort of an unspoken law that you look the other way."

"Well, everybody's good at something," I said. "Do you know Bullwinkle?"

"The moose?" He nodded.

"He had one talent—he could remember everything he had for breakfast since he was born."

"No kidding." He laughed.

Why was he staring over my shoulder?

"See that field?" He pointed behind me.

I turned.

"That belongs to old man Perkins. His scarecrow was stolen—"

"—and a dead man took its place. One of your quaint local customs?"

Abashed, he changed the subject. "By the way, how is your scarecrow?"

I told him about the theft.

Our eyes locked for a second. "Do you think . . . ?"

He shrugged.

"Anyway," I went on, "I have a replacement." And to my astonishment I found myself telling him about Ichabod. When I had finished, I waited tensely for his derisive laugh.

He smiled instead. "I'd like to see him." Then he spoiled it with his next question, "How's the doctor business?"

"It's not a business," I snapped. "Or, at least it shouldn't be," I modified.

"Point taken."

"Sorry." I stuffed the map in my saddlebag. *What's the matter with me? Why am I turning off this perfectly nice guy?* "That's a sore point with me," I explained. "As for doctoring—I don't know if I can make a go of it here. This place isn't exactly overpopulated." I scanned the empty fields. "And the people I've met so far look pretty healthy."

"Wait 'til winter sets in. You'll have plenty of bus . . . er . . . patients. I'll try to steer some your way."

"Don't break your back." *There I go again. Maybe I should see a shrink.* Anxious to get away before I said something worse, I pressed the starter. My bike revved up with a ripple of sound.

His truck, on the other hand, coughed three times, and when it finally caught, backfired. The last I saw of him, he was careening—much too fast—down Possum Hollow Road . . . or was it Crab's Neck?

I trundled along—smooth as silk—and wondered why I didn't feel more satisfaction.

CHAPTER 22

As Thanksgiving neared, I had become as much a fixture in South Jersey as the nuclear cooling tower. My cherry red scarf flapping behind me was as familiar as that cloud of vapor hanging over the tower. As I tore around the neighborhood on my bike, people waved and called out, "Hi, Doc." or "Way to go, Doc!" (Now if I could just get them in the office!) I wondered what would replace my red scarf in the summer months. A red sunbonnet?

I had three invitations for Thanksgiving dinner—from Maggie, from Becca, and, of course, from Dad. But his was only half-hearted. What he was really angling for was an invitation to come to South Jersey and find out what I was up to. I wasn't ready for that.

I couldn't make up my mind which of the other two invitations to accept.

The practice was picking up a little. Locally, I had removed a fishhook, treated a snakebite, and dug a bullet out of a hunter. (He'd shot himself in the foot.) On the motel front, I had treated an acute case of diverticulitis, diagnosed walking pneumonia, and prescribed for the cystitis of half a honeymoon couple. All adults, thank God. On the home front, everything was going smoothly, too. I'd traded the king-size bed in my room for an attractive futon, bought a coffee-grinder and a couple of bright throw rugs.

When (if) my income ever stabilized, I'd buy a rug big enough to cover that whole shit-brown wall-to-wall.

But my office was where I spent most of my time.

Paul, true to his promise, had lent me one of the three cabins in front of the motel to use as an office—rent-free. It was up to me to decorate it, furnish it, and figure out a way to heat it. I chose Cabin 3 because it was in the best condition (which doesn't say much for the other two). When I walked in, the smell of must, mildew, and mouse turds overwhelmed me. There were mouse nests in every corner and spider webs on every windowsill. The walls were bare wood full of knotholes, and there were huge gaps between the floorboards. The toilet had a cracked wooden seat and a chain for flushing—but the last time it had seen water was probably when Noah did. Ditto the sink. I had my work cut out for me. There was electricity, which was good, because it enabled me to work at night. And that's where you could find me most nights, either painting or pounding or paper-hanging. Sometimes I had help from Paul and Jack-the-night-clerk. But more often, it was just advice. One night both of them were there, sitting around joshing me while I worked, until I suggested if they wanted to party, they should try Harry's Bar and Grill. They cast me hurt looks and left. I felt bad afterward. The next night I bought a couple of cases of beer and invited them down. But Maggie got wind of it and said it wouldn't look good for the customers to see the help carousing. And that was the end of it.

Otherwise everything was pretty serene. One of the striking things about this place was the silence, especially as winter approached and the birds headed south. After Manhattan, where horns blew and sirens screamed night and day, this absence of sound was a shock. It was like being tucked inside a box filled with cotton. The racket my bike made was almost a sacrilege. I bought a new muffler and kept the noise to a minimum.

One day I was riding home from a motel call—a woman had burnt her hand on the coffee maker—and the silence was violently shattered. Out of nowhere, the sharp bleat of sirens pierced my ears. I almost ran my bike off the road. What the hell? I stared around me, looking for the source. My eyes were drawn to a black and yellow cone affixed to a stainless steel pole. Oh my God. A leak at the nuclear power plant?

I tore home and burst into the motel lobby. Everything appeared peaceful. No one was rushing around, herding patrons into the cellar. Paul looked up sleepily from his newspaper. "Forget something?"

"The sirens . . ."

"Oh, just a practice session. They do it every month. I should have warned you."

My attempt to look nonchalant was a complete failure. I slumped into a chair to recover.

Paul went back to his newspaper.

Shortly afterward, the nightmares began. They always began with sirens screaming. One night I rushed out of the motel to find people lying all over the parking lot with radiation burns, moaning. I was the only doctor around and all I had to relieve their suffering were the contents of my little medical kit. As I ran from one to the other, I stumbled over something. A bow and an arrow. I picked them up and started shooting the people who were moaning the loudest. When I woke up, I was trembling. This dream recurred with slight variations—I tripped over a shotgun, the people were lying in a field, I couldn't find my medical kit.

The last time it happened, I sat up in bed, turned on all the lights, and remembered some advice my father had once given me: "If you're afraid of something, face it." The occasion had been a Madame Dupont, my high school French teacher, who had picked on me constantly. She terrified me. On my father's advice, I went to see her. "Why don't you like me?" I had asked. She was so embarrassed, she treated me with the greatest respect for the rest of the term.

The next day I made an appointment to tour the nuclear power plant.

• • •

The tour itself was uninspiring. If you've been to an electric generator plant, multiply that a hundred times, add some computers, a few mute employees in green tank suits prowling around, and presto—you'll have a nuclear power plant. The only interesting piece of information provided by our tour guide was: "This plant has the capacity to generate thirty-three million kilowatts of electricity—enough to supply the entire city of New York on an average day." Wow!

The only *jolt* I got was at the end of the tour, when the security guard opened the door to let me out and I recognized him. Mr. Doughboy.

His eyes shifted when I tried to meet them. But it was hardly the place to confront him about an unpaid motel bill. His supervisor, who had also served as the tour guide, was hovering nearby, and I had no desire to get Doughboy fired. He would be in a better position to make good on his debt if he remained employed. I picked up my bike in the parking lot and sped home.

Paul was not even moderately interested in my discovery and adamantly refused to accompany me the next day to follow up on it.

"If I were you, I'd let sleeping dogs lie," he warned, and refused to discuss the subject further.

I thought of mentioning it to Maggie. She had more respect for cold cash than her husband. But in the end, I decided to go alone. By this time, I realized it wasn't the unpaid bill I that bothered me; it was the goon himself. There was something creepy about him.

I planned my visit for the same time as the previous day, hoping Doughboy would be on duty again. But when I arrived at the plant, a different security guard opened the door. Instead of my pudgy, pasty "friend," a slim, attractive woman let me in.

"Where is the guard who was on duty yesterday?" I asked.

She turned to the supervisor who was observing me through his glass booth. "Where is Milac?"

"He quit."

"When?" I asked sharply.

"Last night."

"Did he give any reason?"

"Not to me." He shrugged. "But I think there was some question about his security clearance."

I thought fast. "I'm a friend of his. Could you give me his phone number? I'd like to get in touch with him." *If his phone number was the same as Becca's, I'd know my hunch was right.*

He looked me over. "D'ya have any references?"

I gave him Paul's name and the motel number.

After making the call, he looked at me quizzically. "Your reference wasn't too happy."

"Oh?" I tried to look innocent. "What did he say?"

"Something about 'letting dogs lie.' Who is this Milac—an old boyfriend?" He snickered.

I restrained the desire to punch him. He fumbled through a filing cabinet for a minute. Then he glanced up. "That's funny. His file is missing."

A small shock ran down my spine that had nothing to do with electricity. "How long has he been working here?"

"Under a month. And yesterday he just walked out. No notice. You're supposed to give at least a week's notice."

"Well," I said, "thanks anyway."

The slim woman let me out.

When I barreled up the Sheffield driveway, Becca was sketching in the swing. I stashed my bike and joined her. After admiring her drawing—another falling-down barn—I asked, "Where are your houseguests?"

"Who cares?" She shrugged.

"I do."

Raising her eyes to the field beyond, she said, "There's one of them."

A figure no bigger than an ant was making its way across the horizon. He was carrying something twice his size, which made him look ungainly—like an ant with an enormous breadcrumb.

"What's he doing?"

"Bringing in a scarecrow. It's time. Winter's hard on them."

Spoken like a true farmer. As the tiny, top-heavy figure drew closer to the barn, I jumped up.

"Hey! You just got here," Becca cried.

"Sorry. Gotta go." I was in no mood for a confrontation right now. (Maybe Paul's apathy was contagious.)

As I roared off, I wondered which Milac suffered from constipation. Or was it a family affliction?

CHAPTER 23

Slowly my office was coming into shape. I had repaired all the holes in the floor, and covered my inept carpentry with two colorful rag rugs from the nearest Wal-Mart (twenty-five miles away). I'd painted the shabby woodwork a glossy white, and I'd even papered the waiting room with tiny sprigs of violets on a creamy background. One thing I firmly believed: a doctor's office should be warm and welcoming, like a country inn, not cold and forbidding, like an operating room. People are feeling bad enough when they go to see a doctor. Why make them feel worse?

Maggie was the one who found most of the furniture. She dragged me to local flea markets and yard sales every Saturday morning. She had a knack for spotting a bargain and we made off with some gems. The trick was to arrive early. Real early. Before the dealers. She snagged the rolltop desk right from under the nose of one of the sharpest Philadelphia dealers. (She'd been to so many of these things, she knew all the dealers by sight.) I grabbed the cherry wood coffee table—perfect for all those out-of-date magazines. I found a couple of halfway decent lamps, two soft chairs, and an oak dining table that—with a little padding—became the perfect examining table. You don't want to make the patients too comfortable. They might linger.

But the big find was Maggie's: a pharmacist's chest with cute little drawers for storing pills. I sanded it, buffed it, and stained it. It was my one bona fide antique. When I was done, I went to the local printer and ordered a sign with my office hours and tacked it to the front door. The only thing missing were the patients.

"They'll come," Maggie assured me. "Once the weather changes, they'll come in from their fishing and their hunting and their crabbing and start thinking about their ailments again."

"I sure hope so." I sighed.

It was on one of these furniture jaunts that Maggie confided in me about her son. Except for that day at the auction, when she thought she spied him walking ahead of us, she'd never mentioned Nick. It was the toy train that brought it out.

We were rummaging through a pile of old junk on a table when I heard her catch her breath. I looked up. She was holding a small, black metal steam engine. A wind-up toy. As she turned it over, her eyes filled.

"What is it, Mag?"

"This was Nick's," she said.

"How can you tell?"

She held it out to me and I saw the initials scratched on the bottom. N. N. "He did that with his penknife when he was ten," she said.

"How did it get here?"

She frowned. "He must have sold it. He used to do that, sell his toys—even his clothes—when he . . ." She hesitated. "When he needed money."

She took the train over to the cashier and paid five dollars for it. The expression on her face made me want to cry. She was silent all the way home. I wanted to say something comforting, but nothing came to me. She didn't speak until we were back at the motel. As she pulled into the parking lot, she said. "He had a drug habit, you know."

I shook my head.

"I think that's what happened to him. He overdosed some-where—in the woods, probably—where no one will ever find him." She jerked the key from the ignition. "You see"—she turned toward me—"if he were alive, he would let us know." It was a statement, but her eyes held a question.

What could I say? I didn't know Nick. But from what Tom had told me, I couldn't be sure. My nod seemed to satisfy her.

We went inside and told Paul about all our purchases. All but one.

CHAPTER 24

I decided to grace the Nelsons with my presence on Thanksgiving Day. My dad and I had never made a big thing of that holiday, usually spending it at our favorite diner. Becca would have her aunt and her menial servant (definition of "dogsbody"; I looked it up) and the Milacs for company. But the Nelsons, I reasoned, would probably be celebrating alone.

I couldn't have been more wrong.

The Nelsons lived in a small ranch house a few miles from their motel. As I entered, bearing my hostess gift (it had taken some trouble to find a decent wine around Bayfield—veteran beer country), the delicious aroma of a home-cooked turkey dinner with all the trimmings swept over me. Inhaling deeply, I felt a pang for all those Thanksgiving dinners I had missed.

Maggie gave me a big hug and relieved me of my bottle.

Paul's normally gray countenance was suffused with color as he smiled at me from across the room. The living room was tiny but comfortable, furnished with an ample sofa covered in bright plaid, two homely rocking chairs, and an overstuffed chair that matched the sofa. A rag rug covered most of the floor, and the walls were decorated with old-fashioned samplers. In one corner stood a desk piled high with papers that no one had bothered to hide for the occasion. On the desk was a single framed photograph of a young man with what seemed to me an arrogant expression. Pretending an interest in the sampler above the photo, I moved closer to check him out. I was right. His jaw jutted toward the camera, but his eyes had shifted away from the lens looking to the left. And instead of a smile, his mouth curved in a slight sneer. He didn't resemble either of his parents.

"Work while you work, Play while you play," I read aloud. "Is this your work, Maggie?"

"No, dear. My grandmother made that when she was twelve. Come sit down."

As I obeyed, choosing one of the rockers (I loved rocking chairs), a woman resembling Maggie, but twenty pounds lighter, came in bearing a potted mum. After hugs and kisses were exchanged, she was introduced to me as Polly, Maggie's younger sister. A single woman, she taught eighth grade at the local grammar school.

"How do you do?" She clasped my hand warmly. "I've heard so much about you."

Assuming she had heard about me from the Nelsons, I was surprised when she added, ". . . from Becca."

"Becca?"

"Yes. Becca Borovy. She's a student of mine. A bit unruly right now, but a very talented artist."

"Yes, I know. I've seen some of her drawings."

"I'm trying to steer her toward architecture. She comes by it rightly. She's from Prague, you know."

And two of my most cherished assumptions were wiped out with a single blow. One: Nobody in Bayfield is interested in anything outside of Bayfield. Two: All female children in Bayfield were brought up to cook and sew. Paul handed me a glass of rosy wine, from which I took a large gulp. "I had the same idea," I told the teacher. "I've even promised to take her to New York."

Polly's face lit up almost as much as Becca's had. "Could I come, too?" she asked, instantly smashing my third favorite assumption: Everyone in Bayfield hates New York.

"Sure," I agreed eagerly. "Let's set a date right now. How about—" I was cut off by the doorbell.

"Oh, that must be Tom," Maggie said, and Paul went to answer it.

"Tom?" I asked no one in particular.

"Tom Canby," Polly said, as a male voice rose in the hall.

I turned to see Paul usher Robin Hood into the living room.

CHAPTER 25

"You know Maggie's sister, Polly." Mr. Nelson was doing the honors. "And this is Jo Banks, our new doctor." His tone of veneration made me want to crawl under the coffee table.

"Dr. Banks and I have met," Tom said.

"Oh? Where?"

If he said Harry's Bar & Grill I'd slug him.

"On the road. She was a bit confused by our lack of road signs."

Paul chuckled. "Well, I'm sure you set her straight."

Throughout this little exchange, I maintained a fixed smile.

"Hello, Tommy. Give me a kiss." Maggie appeared from the kitchen, hair awry, wearing an apron and holding a bottle of wine. "Time for just one more before dinner." She began filling each of our glasses to the brim.

General conversation resumed. I didn't have to speak directly to Tom until we were crowding into the little hall that led to the dining room. He was right behind me.

"Are you white meat or dark?" He spoke over my shoulder.

I shrugged.

"I'd take you for dark."

He was right, of course. "Wrong," I said.

"I'll be darned. Full of surprises."

I surprised myself. Why had I lied to him?

The process of squeezing into chairs around the small table absorbed all our attention. The turkey rested in solitary splendor on a platter on the sideboard. Everyone admired its fat legs and glistening brown skin. The other dishes were crowded in the center of the table. Stuffing, sweet potatoes, creamed corn, onions, green beans with almonds, coleslaw, cranberry sauce, applesauce . . . it went on and on.

"Pay special attention to my oyster stuffing," Maggie said. "It's made with local oysters. This is the first year we've been allowed to eat them since the blight of 'seventy-nine."

I found myself seated with Polly on my right and Paul's empty chair on my left. Maggie was at the other end of the table, and Tom sat across from me. This was annoying, because every time I looked up I would catch him staring at me. But it was better than having to make conversation with him. I began talking animatedly to Polly about our forthcoming trip to New York.

"We can drive over early in the morning—" I stopped.

"What's wrong?"

"No car. All I have is my bike. And I can't see the three of us making it on that!" I grimaced.

"You can borrow my pickup," Tom offered with a wry grin.

"Very funny." A pickup in New York would stand out like a yellow cab in Bayfield.

"Don't worry," Polly said. "I have a car. But you have to promise to do all the city driving. I'd have a heart attack."

"Jo."

I looked up.

Paul was standing by the turkey, waving his carving knife at me. "White or dark?"

"Dark, please."

As I turned back to Polly, I caught Tom's triumphant grin.

Damn him.

"Then, after we dump the car," I plowed on, ignoring him, "we can have breakfast at this great deli—"

"Corned beef and rye for breakfast?" Tom looked askance.

"—where they have great omelets," I finished.

He snorted into his napkin.

When everyone had been presented with a plate containing his or her meat preference, it was time to hand round the other dishes. Quite a production.

"Now don't hang back, folks, there's plenty more of everything in the kitchen," Maggie urged.

By the time we had finished serving ourselves, my pink china plate was completely covered. About to dig in, I was suddenly conscious of an awkward pause. Everyone was looking expectantly at Paul, who had taken his seat at the head of the table. He was staring at his plate, his expression stony. Maggie waited a moment longer before she rapidly said grace.

Why did I feel this overwhelming sense of relief—as if some dreadful crisis had been averted?

The "amen" acted as a starting bell, and everyone dug in.

Completely immersed in the enjoyment of this incredible dinner, I forgot my stupid blunder about the meat. I even forgot Tom. It certainly was different from the diner, even from Manhattan's most expensive gourmet restaurants. You couldn't buy food like this. It just wasn't available.

During dinner, the story of the twenty-year oyster blight was gone over in minute detail. This led to talk of pollution and the threat of the power plant. "It's destroying the fish and crabs," Paul said. "They're dying every day because of the hot water pumped from the plant into the streams and creeks." A discussion of Cohansey Creek and its history followed. "Back in Colonial times, these coves and inlets were full of pirates," Tom said, looking at me. "And they're supposed to hold buried treasure."

Maggie mentioned seeing wild turkeys. A flock of them had crossed the road in front of her, and one of them had been an albino! Tom had seen them, too. Apparently, the area had been full of wild turkeys once, until 1982 when they had suddenly disappeared. Now they were back. Wow! Had anyone wired the *Times*?

When the pumpkin pie appeared, with a side dish of real whipped cream, my stomach groaned. But somehow, I managed to stuff in a piece before we finally rose and moved back into the living room.

I had made my plans—stick close to Polly—to avoid any more encounters with Tom. *What the hell is your problem? He's damned attractive. Are you nuts?* My worries were needless. The party split along traditional gender lines—the men in one corner discussing the merits of the hunting season; the women in the other, discussing everything else.

"I overheard you talking about Becca Borovy earlier," Maggie began, settling down with a bag bulging with knitting. "Aren't her people foreigners?"

"They're from Czechoslovakia," Polly said, "or rather, the Czech Republic now."

"They *were* foreigners," I inserted. "They died when Becca was four."

"Oh?" Polly turned to me. "I didn't know that. I thought her parents had just sent her over here to get her away from the Communists."

"It seems her grandfather is still alive, and when her parents died he sent Becca to live with her aunt."

"Poor child. No wonder she's a bit rebellious. Although her aunt seems decent enough. Have you met her?" Polly asked.

I nodded.

Maggie was rapidly slipping stitches onto a new knitting needle. She interrupted her counting to ask, "Isn't there some man living with them?"

"Yes. Juri."

"Juri? What a funny name." Maggie went back to her counting.

"Not really. It's as common as Jack or . . . Tom . . . in their country." I had no idea if this was true, but it riled me when people talked about "foreigners."

"Did you meet him?" asked Maggie.

I nodded.

"Who is he? What does he do?" Polly, this time. "I've seen him around the Sheffield place, dressed like a farmhand. He's such a handsome fella."

I smiled. It always surprised me when people over forty noticed things like that. But then, Juri was probably about Polly's age. "According to Becca, he's a relative and acts as their handyman."

"What did you think of him?" Maggie again, knitting at a sixty-mile-an-hour clip.

"He seemed okay. A bit nosy. But . . ."

"Nosy?" Maggie was not beyond nosy herself.

"Oh, he asked a whole lot of questions about my medical education, my practice in New York, where and how I was going to practice here . . . I guess I was supersensitive. This was a few days after I'd decided to stay, and I didn't have all the answers myself." I was suddenly aware of silence on the male side of the room. Paul was smoking his pipe with a contemplative expression, but Tom was blatantly listening to me. He got up quickly and came over.

"How is the practice going?" he asked, very politely.

"Fine, thank you." Equally polite.

"I see you now and then. Your red scarf is like a bright flag. It's nice to see a spot of color this time of year."

"There's always the winter wheat," I retorted.

"True." His smile vanished. He turned to Maggie, "That was some feast you laid on us, lady." He bent and kissed her. "I'm going to try and walk it off now. Many thanks."

I was sure he had planned to ask me to join him on his walk, and was turned off by my rudeness. I was torn between relief and regret. To my dismay, I realized regret had taken the lead.

After Tom left, the party began to sag. Polly yawned. Paul openly dozed in his chair. Maggie began to collect the dirty wine glasses. I offered to help with the dishes but was quickly rebuffed.

"Not on your life. That's what dishwashers are for. I'm not going to touch those things 'til tomorrow."

"Oh, Mag, you have to at least rinse them," her sister said. "And what about the pots? Let us help."

"No." She stared us both down with her most severe, admitting-no-nonsense Mary Poppins glare. We subsided and Maggie disappeared into the kitchen.

"I'm so glad we met," I said to Polly. "Maybe you could give me your phone number in case I come up with some new ideas for our trip."

"Of course." She reached in her bag for paper and pen. "We never did set a date," she reminded me, handing me the number.

We both took out our date books and settled on December 14.

"I'll take care of contacting Becca," I said. Turning to say good-bye to Paul, I found him still sound asleep. As I started off to find Maggie, I glanced at the picture on the desk once more. Polly caught my glance.

"That's Nick," she spoke in a low tone, and came nearer.

"He doesn't look like either of them," I said.

"He was adopted."

"Oh."

"He . . ."

Thinking she was going to tell me about his disappearance, I said, "I know he's . . . gone."

She nodded, looking grave. "This is the first Thanksgiving they've celebrated since . . ." She paused. "I think you had something to do with that. They were afraid you wouldn't have any place to go."

So I *had* picked the right invitation.

"Did you notice that Paul wouldn't say grace today?" Polly continued. "Maggie had to say it. Paul made a bargain with God, you know?"

I shook my head.

"If God brought his son back, he would go to church every Sunday."

"And?"

"And—if He didn't, Paul would never set foot inside a church again." Polly, apparently a church person, frowned. "That was three years ago. And he never has."

Not having been in a church for much longer than that, I didn't know what to say. Fortunately Paul woke up and Maggie came in from the kitchen. I said my thanks and good-byes to everyone and left.

It was twilight when I emerged from the snug house. The vast expanse of ever-changing sky never failed to surprise me. Encumbered by a skirt, pantyhose, and heels, I boarded my bike more awkwardly than usual. And once settled, I drove more slowly, taking in the sky. It was a creamy yellow—the color of the corn we'd had for dinner. It spread around me like a giant comforter, threatening to defrost that frozen lump inside my chest that passed for a heart. *Whoa! Too much wine? Or too much turkey?*

A flock of geese stitched their way across the sky in swift, straight lines and disappeared. By the time I reached the motel, it had turned deep lavender and a few stars had broken out.

Jack-the-night-clerk was on duty.

"Happy Thanksgiving," I said.

He looked up from his tattered paperback, *Return of the Jedi,* and gave me a brief smile.

"I didn't know there were so many *Star Wars* books," I said.

"There aren't. I reread them."

With a twinge of guilt I wondered where he had had his Thanksgiving dinner. Or *if* he'd had one. I resolved to take more interest in Jack.

As I trudged up the stairs to my room, I felt weighed down by more than the heavy meal I'd just eaten. Instead of being buoyed up by the party, I was let down. Why was that? Later, while I undressed and got ready for bed, I tried to analyze my feelings. After all, I was a doctor—and I *had* taken a few psychiatry courses.

First, there was the photo of Nick on the desk. As I'd studied his cold, arrogant expression, I'd felt a chill in that warm living room. Then there was the awkward pause before dinner, when Paul had refused to say grace—even though it was a day especially set aside for giving thanks and his wife's eyes were fixed on him beseechingly. Then there was my own weird behavior with Tom. For some reason I couldn't relax and enjoy him—even though he had gone way out of his way to be friendly. Why? It was as if I was punishing myself. For what? Slowly it came to me, oozing up from my soul like sour mud from the river bottom. Sophie. I can never be happy until I forgive myself for her death. Stunned by my insight, I sat on the edge of the bed, staring down at my feet, not seeing them. I sighed. Well, Freud would be proud of me.

The last thing I remember before falling asleep was Tom's face when I'd snapped, "There's always the Winter Wheat!" His expression was a comical mix of bewilderment and—hurt. But somehow I didn't feel like laughing.

CHAPTER 26

The worst part of office hours was I had to wear a skirt. As I approached my newly rehabbed cabin I was surprised to see Becca straddling her bike, beside the door.

"You're late." She pointed to the new sign displaying my office hours:

MON., WED. & FRI.
2:00 TO 4:00 P.M.

"Sorry." I checked my watch. Five past two. I didn't tell her I had so few patients I didn't feel compelled to rush to the office. It was my motel clients that kept me solvent. But I had this secret yearning for private patients, too. Some practice I could call my own. Very old-fashioned.

"What's wrong?" I unlocked the door. "You look pretty healthy."

Becca followed me inside without answering. She was quiet while I changed into my white coat, washed my hands, and sat down behind my desk. She remained standing, or rather, lounging against the doorjamb, until I said, "Won't you sit down?"

She plopped into the empty chair across from me.

I waited.

Avoiding my eyes, she muttered to the floor, "I want to go on the pill."

I was silent for so long, she finally glanced up.

"You're only thirteen," I said.

"So? Girls in Shakespeare's time married at thirteen."

Romeo and Juliet must be on the curriculum at Bayfield Junior High. "When did you start your period?"

"Six months ago."

I stared out the window, chewing my pencil. "Why do you want to go on the pill?"

Her eyebrows shot up. "Don't you know where babies come from?"

I wanted to slap her. Controlling myself, I said pleasantly, "You know, there are a lot of diseases out there."

She smiled patronizingly. "Not if you use protection."

"And who's the lucky fellow?" I couldn't prevent the unprofessional question.

She shrugged.

I took a prescription pad from my drawer. The only thing Becca needed less than the pill was a baby. Carefully I wrote the prescription, tore it off, and handed it to her.

"Thanks." She tucked it into the pocket of her jeans, but she seemed in no hurry to leave. "Something funny's going on at my house," she blurted.

I was all ears.

"You know that refugee couple who came over from Prague a while ago?"

I nodded, although I didn't know they were from Praque.

"There's nothing special about that. My aunt's always taking in strays from Europe, letting them stay with us until they get on their feet, as she says."

"That's very kind of her."

"There used to be more of them, before the Velvet Revolution. Now there's not so many . . ."

I didn't interrupt.

"But this couple's different . . ."

"In what way?"

She frowned. "They're mean."

"How?"

"They're always watching me. And they tell tales on me. If they catch me coming in late or eating between meals, they rat on me. They tell my aunt, and then she grounds me."

It was my turn to raise my eyebrows.

"And once . . . the woman slapped me."

I flinched. Then I remembered having the same urge about two minutes ago.

"And they're always whispering in corners, together or with Juri. My aunt doesn't seem to notice."

She wouldn't, I thought. *She's in another world.*

"I think it's rude."

"It is."

"Besides . . ." she added, with the shadow of a smile, "I want to know what they're talking about."

"So would I."

"But that's not the worst part . . ."

She had my full attention.

"Yesterday, when I came home from school and went into the barn—I do that sometimes after school. It's quiet there and smells good."

I nodded, understanding. I used to seek out a quiet place after the noise and turmoil of school. But we didn't have a barn. I went to my room.

"I was sitting there, not doing anything, when the floor started to rise up right in front of me."

"The floor of the barn?"

She nodded. "It was a trapdoor. I'd never noticed it before. It had been covered with packed down mud and hay. Anyway, Mr. Pie Face . . . that's what I call him, 'cause he has this pudgy, pushed-in face . . ."

"Go on."

"Then I remembered my uncle talking once about a bomb shelter. His father had built it in the fifties, when there was an A-bomb scare. And I wondered if that was where the trapdoor led. Anyway, after Pie Face got over the shock of seeing me, he climbed out, grabbed my arm, and twisted it behind my back. When I started to yell, he covered my mouth with his sweaty hand." Becca physically recoiled at the memory. "Then he hissed in my ear, 'Tell anybody about this and I'll break your arm!' " And he gave my arm an extra twist." She winced and rubbed her arm. "It still hurts."

"Let's see." I stepped quickly around my desk to examine her arm. It showed no obvious sign of a break. "Can you bend your elbow?"

She did.

"You'll live," I said. "But," I added, "I'm going to look into this."

"No." Becca turned white. "You mustn't tell him I told you."

"But your aunt has to know about it." My adrenaline had been steadily rising during this conversation. Now it was rapidly reaching its peak.

"No. Please, Jo." The panic in her eyes startled me.

"I can't let you go back to an abuser!"

"I'll . . . I'll call you if it happens again. I promise."

"What if you can't get to a phone?"

She pulled a cell phone from her back pocket. Cell phones were not as common in Bayfield as in Manhattan, but Becca had a slim, silver, lightweight, state-of-the-art model.

As I hesitated for a second, thinking, Becca darted toward the door.

"Wait."

Cold air brushed my ankles. She had the door open.

"Could you get your aunt to ask me for dinner again?"

She turned with a smile. "Sure." The smile died. "I mean . . . I don't know . . ."

"What do you mean?"

"Lately, Juri doesn't like visitors."

I wasn't about to let her go. "What if I just happen to drop by tonight, say around dinnertime?"

She grinned. For a split second she looked like Sophie—or, how Sophie might have looked at thirteen. I watched her hop on her bike and take off as if she hadn't a care in the world.

Had she really wanted the pill, or was that just an excuse to tell me about Milac?

CHAPTER 27

Since patients weren't breaking my door down, I spent the rest of my office hours reading journals. I was about to call it a day when a pickup truck pulled into the parking lot behind the cabin. A burly man in jeans and a windbreaker got out. He looked cautiously left and right before coming to the door. This was unusual. I'd had very few male patients since I'd opened my office. They sent their wives, their children, and their mothers, but they didn't come themselves. *What kind of a guy would go to a woman doctor?* was the general attitude.

He came into the waiting room, looking around uncertainly. Until I could afford a secretary, I acted as my own. Stepping from my office, I said, "May I help you? I'm Dr. Banks."

He looked nonplussed and I'm sure his first instinct was to run.

"How did you hear about me?" I asked.

"My brother . . ." he grimaced. Obviously he guessed his brother had played a prank on him—sending him, unawares, to a woman doctor.

Since the fish was nibbling, I decided to give him more line. "What's your name?"

"Jake. Jake Potter."

"Won't you take off your jacket, Mr. Potter?"

Slowly he unzipped his windbreaker. After removing it he

looked for a place to hang it. I took it from him and hung it on the handsome clothes tree Maggie and I had snagged for a song at a yard sale.

"Please step this way."

His eyes scanned the room, still searching for a way out. By sheer force of will, I reeled him into my inner office. He sat on the edge of his chair.

From the other side of my desk, I asked, "What seems to be the trouble?"

Resigned, like a condemned man, he cleared his throat. "I have these dreams. . . ."

Ohmygod. He thinks I'm a psychiatrist. "What sort of dreams?"

"Nightmares!" *Once hooked, the fish was cooperating.*

I assumed my most sympathetic expression. *A patient is a patient is a patient.* "About what, Mr. Potter?" I adopted my most reassuring tone.

"About the body I found."

Ohmygod—was he a psychopath? I kept my cool. "When was this, Mr. Potter?"

"Didn't you read about it? It was in all the papers. I was even on TV!"

"Oh, *that* body," I said quickly. (*So this was the guy who found the scarecrow—that wasn't a scarecrow. Interesting.*) "Do they know how he got there?"

He shook his head. "But he was drugged and hung out there to die. If I hadn't found him, the buzzards woulda picked his bones clean." He shuddered involuntarily.

"It's only natural, after such an experience, that you would have some after effects," I said soothingly.

"I can't sleep," he said.

On closer examination, he did look exhausted. Deep shadows lay under his eyes, and beneath his farmer's tan I suspected a pasty complexion.

"I thought maybe you could give me a pill."

A pill—that magic solution to all problems. "What do you do each night before you go to bed?" *Bad question; he probably peed.* I hastily rephrased it. "I mean, what's your nightly routine?"

"Oh, me an' the boys go out to the Anchor an' have a few beers, play some pool, listen to the jukebox . . . you know . . ."

"And when you come home?"

He looked puzzled. "I go to bed."

"Don't you ever take a hot bath? Listen to some soft music? Maybe read a book . . . ?"

He stared.

"Well, that's what I want you to do tonight. Instead of going to the Anchor, I want you to stay home. Watch TV until about nine o'clock." (I was going to suggest a glass of warm milk, but I didn't want to scare him to death.) "Then take a long, hot bath. Soak in the tub for about half an hour. Then get into bed. Read a magazine or look at the newspaper, until you start to doze off."

"How 'bout a comic book?"

"Fine."

"No pill?"

I went to the medicine chest, shook some Tylenol into an envelope, and gave them to him. "Take two before your bath."

Relieved, he stowed the envelope in his pocket.

"And if all else fails, Mr. Potter . . ."

He looked up expectantly.

". . . you can always think about pretty girls."

He chuckled. "What d' I owe you?"

"Twenty dollars."

He pulled out a roll of bills and peeled one off. As he reached for his windbreaker, I said, "Let me know how you make out."

"Yes, ma'am." His words had the ring of sincerity.

I was jubilant. I'd landed a new patient! But the memory of the body in the field sobered me. Not everything in Bayfield was peaceful and serene. I locked up and checked my watch. Just time to freshen up for my impromptu dinner engagement at Becca's.

CHAPTER 28

As I tooled up the driveway of the Sheffield farm, I saw Juri working on the porch. He had returned to his farmhand role. In old jeans, a faded work shirt, and thick work boots, all signs of the dapper houseman had disappeared. Some of the screening had come loose around the porch door and he was tacking it back.

"Hi," I shouted over the rumble of my motor. "Becca around?"

He shook his head, continuing to pound.

"When will she be back?"

He shrugged.

I was getting anxious.

He stopped pounding. "She and her aunt took a trip."

"A trip?" I shut off the motor. "I just saw her."

"I drove them to the airport this afternoon."

"Where'd they go?"

"Florida."

"Florida? For how long? What about school?"

He looked up, annoyed. "She has tutors," he snapped.

I got the message. Becca's education was none of my business.

"When will she be back?"

"In a few weeks." He stuck the hammer into the pocket of an apron-belt contraption he wore around his waist.

"By the fourteenth?"

He looked wary. "What's the fourteenth?"

"Oh, nothing. Just a little excursion we'd planned."

"I doubt it."

"Will she be back by Christmas?" We could always go the week after Christmas. The decorations would still be up and there'd still be a festive air.

He had turned to go into the house. "Don't count on it," he tossed over his shoulder and disappeared inside.

I fluctuated between relief and alarm. At least Becca was out of the house and away from that creep Milac. But it was so sudden. She hadn't mentioned anything about a trip. Her aunt must have been packed and ready to go when the kid returned from my office. Strange. If Becca weren't her niece, I'd call it kidnapping. Maybe her otherworldly aunt had suddenly caught on that her niece was being harassed, and decided to remove her from the scene. That would be the best scenario.

I sat staring at the closed, forbidding house. Shades were pulled down over the tall windows, hiding the old glass and creamy white curtains. Two wicker rockers were tipped forward against the wall of the house, their backs turned to me. And the porch swing was shrouded in a dark green canvas cover.

I was about to take off when I spotted the corner of Becca's sketchbook, sticking out from under the swing. It might get wet if it rained. I dismounted, and went up on the porch. For some reason, I walked quietly, almost tiptoeing. I even glanced over my shoulder once. I snatched up the book, and instead of stashing it on the swing—it would have been perfectly safe under the canvas cover—I tucked it inside the front of my jacket. With more furtive glances, I mounted my bike and took off.

CHAPTER 29

I slid Becca's sketchbook into my bureau drawer and tried not to think about her. What could I do? Her aunt—and legal guardian—had taken her on a trip. What was so bad about that? At least she was out of town, and away from that slimeball Milac. The next few days were so busy, I had little time to worry about Becca.

As soon as I returned from the Sheffield Farm, there was a knock on my door. I opened it to Maria, one of the chamber-maids, who was in great distress. Timidly she held up a finger in which a splinter about the size of an ant was lodged. It was so small I didn't bother taking her down to my official office. "Come on in. I can take care of that right here." I ushered her into my emergency office, pulled down the toilet lid, and seated her on it. Then I went to get my medical kit. When I reappeared holding a syringe she started to scream. Fortunately I knew no Spanish, so her curses bounced off me like dandelion puffs. Calmly, I dismantled the needle and explained to her that I had no intention of giving her a shot. I only wanted to use the syringe as a probe to get the splinter out. She was quiet for thirty seconds—until I moved toward her with the needle. Then she started up again. You would think I was about to amputate. And the reverberations in that tile bathroom! Inspired by her screams, I removed the splinter with a deftness—one flick—I didn't know I possessed. When I showed it to Maria, the transformation was magical; her tear-stained face broke into a radiant smile. I swabbed her finger with cotton soaked in alcohol and applied a Band-Aid. She reached into the pocket of her uniform, looking at me inquiringly.

I shook my head.

"*Gracias!*" She hugged me.

But when I offered her the splinter as a souvenir, she shrieked and ran out of the room.

I had barely finished cleaning up after Maria when the phone rang. It was Mike, from the garage. He had to identify himself because his voice was unrecognizable. It was the voice of a man thirty years his senior. "I think I have the flu," he croaked.

"Don't move," I said. "I'm coming over."

Mike's apartment was on top of his garage. It was bright and cheerful, neat and tidy. Why was I surprised that a bachelor's quarters were not a pigsty? Reverse discrimination? Completely buried beneath a dark blue comforter, he greeted me with a weak moan.

"When did this begin?" I pulled a chair up to the side of the bed and took out my stethoscope.

"Thanksgiving."

"Too much turkey?"

"Nah." He managed to sound indignant.

I asked him to sit up. He was wearing no pajama top. I wasn't about to investigate for bottoms. When I pressed the stethoscope to his bare back, he flinched.

"Why don't you ever warm those things up?"

"Shhhh." I was hearing definite rales. I switched the stethoscope to his chest. More rales. I took out the earplugs. "Why don't you wear any clothes in November?"

He grunted and slid back under the comforter.

I took out a thermometer, shook it down to 96 degrees, popped it under his tongue, and checked my watch. "Now I can read you the riot act without interruption. You have severe bronchitis that could easily become pneumonia. I'm going to give you a strong antibiotic. But that won't cure you by itself. You must drink lots of fluids and get plenty of bed rest."

He sat back up. "I have a garage to run, lady."

"Do you want to be out of commission for a month?" I stared him back down under the covers. "Now shut up and do what the doctor tells you." I took out the thermometer: 103 degrees. "And I'll need a chest X ray."

He groaned.

"Do you have any help?" I thought I'd seen some boys working around the place.

"Kids." He shrugged. "They're okay when I'm around. But without me they're worthless."

I nodded. "My father had the same problem. But then, he had me." Memories of late nights working as a printer's devil came back to me. The smell of ink and freshly cut paper. Not unpleasant memories. I could have been happy as a printer.

"Would you like to apply for the job?" He croaked and immediately launched into a coughing fit.

"Seriously." I glared at him. "Either you get help or you close up until this is over." I set a bottle of pills on his bedside table. "Two now, and one a day until they're all gone."

He returned my glare.

"Cheer up." I clicked my kit shut. "It's not the end of the world."

He started to get out of bed.

"Hey . . ." (He *was* wearing bottoms.)

"There's some cash in the top drawer over there." He pointed to a bureau on the other side of the room. "Take what I owe you."

I opened the drawer and took a ten and a twenty from a greasy pile. I held up the two bills. "Ten for the antibiotic; twenty for the house call."

He nodded.

"Want a receipt?"

"Yeah. I better. Taxes."

I wrote out a receipt, and signed it.

He sat up to reach for it and fell back exhausted.

"See what I mean?"

He managed a faint grin.

As I started to let myself out, he said hoarsely, "Stop any bullets lately?"

I paused. "Not lately."

"That's good." He shut his eyes and rolled himself up in his comforter.

"Don't forget that X ray," I reminded him.

"Omph."

I closed the door softly behind me.

My next call was quite different. Paul handed me the phone message as I came in the door. The address was a posh motor inn in the heart of Wilmington with ninety-five units. I happened to know they charged $200-plus a night. The message read, "Female guest with possible broken ankle. Refuses X ray."

Great. Did she think I was Superman with X ray vision?

It took almost an hour to get there—over the Delaware Memorial Bridge, down 1-95, into the business center of Wilmington—fighting traffic all the way. But I had no trouble finding it. Its only competition was the regal Hotel du Pont, a few blocks away. RODNEY MOTOR INN, the electric marquee gleamed against the sky. Caesar Rodney had been one of the signers of the Declaration of Independence. I had a vague memory that he had arrived in the final hour and saved the day.

Pulling into the parking lot, I bypassed the red-coated parking valet, found a space on my own, and locked up my bike. As I trudged toward the entrance, I was suddenly conscious of my jeans, my black leather jacket, and my boots. The outfit had cost me an arm and a leg, but they clashed with the decor. An elegant middle-aged couple in evening togs preceded me through the door. I zipped past the doorman and into the lobby, resisting the impulse to shield my eyes against the glitter. Wall-to-wall brass and glass. I wondered how this place could call itself a motel. Some tax loophole, no doubt. The man behind the desk stared blatantly at me. I marched up to him.

"Dr. Banks." I spoke briskly, looking him straight in the eye. "Your manager called me about a guest with a possible ankle fracture."

"Oh, yes. A Mrs. Ferguson." He waved a bellhop over. "Will you escort this lady to room nine-thirteen?"

"I don't need an escort. Just point me to the elevators."

The bellhop slunk back to his corner.

"Certainly. Straight ahead and to your right." He couldn't resist a disdainful glance at my jeans and boots.

"And the powder room?" I said. "I'd like to change first."

His expression of relief was funny. He pointed to a sign: REST ROOMS.

Appropriately attired in a skirt, blouse, pantyhose and flats, I returned to the front desk. The desk clerk didn't recognize me.

"Can you store this for me?" I pushed my backpack bulging with biking boots, jeans, jacket, and helmet across the counter.

Recognition dawned. "Oh, certainly." He whisked my bag under the counter as if it contained an especially virulent strain of Legionnaire's disease.

As I headed for the elevators, I heard him dial a number and say, "Mrs. Ferguson, Dr. Banks is on her way up."

The ride to the ninth floor was swift and silent, reminding me of the Trump Tower on Fifth Avenue. God, that seemed a thousand miles away. Soundlessly, the doors slid open and I stepped into pile like deep snow. But instead of white, it was pale gold. I found Room 913 and knocked.

An immaculately groomed CEO type in a dark suit opened the door. "Dr. Banks?"

Who did he think? The chambermaid? I wasn't carrying sheets or towels. I nodded.

He stepped aside.

I had an impression of more pale gold with white accents. Usually, when attending a patient, their surroundings remained a blur until I made my diagnosis. Only then could I focus on unessential details. But this was different. The details hit me over the head.

Mrs. Ferguson, in a black negligée, was stretched out on a white sofa, her ailing foot elevated by a pillow and wrapped in a gold towel. A tumbler half-filled with a dark liquid stood on a glass table at her side. A lighted cigarette rested in the crystal ashtray. With a guilty look, she crushed it out. An old-fashioned lady.

Without waiting for more introductions, I asked, "How did this happen?" and began unpacking my kit.

She glanced at her male companion for help. (Mr. Ferguson?)

"Last night." Whoever-He-Was spoke for her. "We were coming home from the theater and she tripped on the doorsill in the lobby."

Uh-oh. No wonder the desk clerk was nervous. We were talking major lawsuit material.

"We were both a bit tipsy," Mrs. Ferguson added with a sheepish smile.

So much for lawsuits. "Let's have a look." I bent to examine the ankle. It was quite swollen. When I applied gentle pressure, the woman jerked away and gave a little yelp.

"Sorry," I muttered. Pampered crybaby women did nothing to improve my bedside manner. "This should be X rayed immediately," I said, happy to tell her what I knew she least wanted to hear. "You could have saved me a trip by just going to the hospital in the first place."

The lady cast another look at Mr. Whosis.

"We'd rather avoid the hospital in a strange place," he said.

"The Delaware Medical Center has an excellent reputation."

"Could you possibly strap it temporarily so she could get home to her own doctor?"

"Where is home?"

"Washington, D.C."

I frowned. "It should be X rayed right away. If it's broken, the longer it's not in a cast, the more likely . . ." I stopped. No point scaring her to death. "Did you drive?"

He nodded.

"All right," I shrugged, guessing from his manner and attire that he owned the last word in comfortable vehicles. "It's against my better judgment, but I'll strap it for you."

The twosome exchanged another look, and I felt their relief balloon around me.

I worked silently, wrapping the ankle. No small talk to lighten things up. I was too irritated. Except for a wince or two, the woman bore up better than I'd expected. When I had finished, I asked if she'd taken anything for the pain.

"Only aspirin."

I rummaged in my kit for some Motrin. "Take two now, and a third later, if the pain increases." I was about to write out a bill with a receipt. These types usually had ample insurance. But he stopped me.

"What is your fee?"

I blinked, thought briefly of doubling it, decided against it. "Fifty," I said.

He had his billfold out and was handing me two crisp twenties and a ten.

"I'll give you a receipt so your insurance company can reimburse . . ."

"That won't be necessary."

"But—"

"We appreciate your coming." He pointed me toward the door.

As I plowed through the plush carpeting toward the elevator, I mused on the inconvenience of accidents when one is engaged in a clandestine affair.

CHAPTER 30

It was nearly midnight as I approached Bayfield. And cold. That last call had left a bad taste in my mouth. Not because of my patient and her boyfriend; I was no prude. It was the setting. All that glitz. And the knowledge that most of my colleagues would think nothing of spending one or two nights there didn't help my mood. The contrast between the gaudy decor of the Rodney Motor Inn and the scene before me was startling. Bare fields. Empty sky. Clean, cold air sweeping through me like a broom.

Uh-oh. A barrier of orange cones like witches' hats blocked the entrance to the little concrete bridge that I usually took over Stow Creek. And there was a new sign: DETOUR. I turned right and peered through the darkness for the next sign. There wasn't one. After a few miles I turned left, then left again. Logically, this should return me to the direction I wanted to go. Another few miles revealed no familiar landmarks. Don't tell me, after all these weeks, I had managed to get lost—again?

I slowed down, searching the landscape. No landmarks. No buildings. No scarecrows. Just field and sky and road. Not even an abandoned barn. Only a vision of Tom Canby with his impudent grin, mocking me. I gave the grip on my right handlebar a twist, throwing open the throttle. Maybe around the next bend . . .

A house, buried among tall trees. I slowed and peered up the weedy driveway. Pickup truck parked at an angle. Dark windows. No sign of habitation. Not even a dog barking. Oh, well. I turned in and parked next to the truck. As I got out, I ran my hand over the hood. Still warm. Where was the driver? Inside? My boots cracked like gun shots on the wooden porch. My knocks rang out loudly.

Silence.

Did I mention the winter silence? Complete absence of sound. In the fall, there were the geese. And sometimes, even now, there was a wind. But usually there was nothing. Like tonight. Except for whatever noise I made—with my feet, hands, or breath. I knocked again. The knocks dropped into the stillness like stones into a well.

I moved away from the door, treading as softly as possible on the wooden steps. As I started for my bike, I heard someone slide out of the cab of the truck behind me.

I got on the bike and fumbled for the ignition. He jumped on me and tried to wrestle me to the ground. I found the ignition. He was on the back of my bike. My motor started up. He clamped his arms around my waist, trying to rock me loose. His hands moved up my arms, to my shoulders—reaching for my neck. His fingers tightened around my throat. I twisted the handlebar grip and popped a wheelie. The nose of my bike surged through the air.

His fingers slipped. He hit the ground a little before my front wheel did. Without looking back, I gave the grip a vicious twist, accelerating to the highest possible speed—over a hundred miles per hour. The noise of the bike ripped the winter silence to shreds.

Fear, like a vacuum cleaner, sucked my brain clean of everything except what I needed to find my way home. The glowing orange sign—OAKVIEW MOTOR LODGE—showed up by the side of the road like a jack-in-the-box. I had no idea how it got there. How *I* got there. But it wasn't until I parked my bike and dismounted that I realized the full extent of my fear. My legs wouldn't work. I tottered like a drunk to the door of the motel and had to steady myself against the doorjamb before I went in.

I could have gone straight to my room, but I needed to hear a human voice. A friendly human voice. *I'll just pop in and say good night to Jack,* I thought.

What met my eyes was completely unexpected. Instead of finding Jack hunched over the desk, keeping his lonely vigil in a solitary pool of light, the lobby was full of people, lights blazed, and Jack was nowhere to be seen. Paul and Maggie, their backs to me, were hovering above a third person who was seated. When they heard me come in, they both whipped around. "Thank God!" Paul said.

How could he possibly have known about my attack?

"Come quick. This boy's cut himself bad." Stepping aside, Paul allowed me a view of the third person—a boy, around nine or ten—slumped on the vinyl sofa. Grimly, Maggie held a towel to his wrist with both hands. The towel was scarlet. So was the boy's T-shirt, pants, and the carpet under his feet.

I can't do this, I thought. Then I sprinted forward and tore open my kit. "Did you call nine-one-one?"

"They're on their way," Paul said.

I yanked out a rubber tourniquet and wrapped it tightly around the boy's arm, just below the elbow. "Can you hold on a little longer, Maggie?"

She nodded.

"I'd switch with you, but it would be risky."

She shook her head and increased her grip on the boy's wrist.

"How did it happen?" I asked the boy.

"Piece of glass in the parking lot."

"What's your name?"

"Bryan."

"Where are your parents, Bryan?"

"In their room." For the first time he looked scared. "Don't wake them—please. They told me to get lost."

"At midnight? In the parking lot?"

He looked sheepish. "No. That was my idea."

Where is that G.D. ambulance? "What's your room number?"

"I . . . forget."

I glanced at Paul. He went to the desk, rummaged a minute, and disappeared.

"Are you okay?" I asked Maggie, quietly.

Her nod was slower this time.

I moved my hands under hers. "When I say 'now,' let go."

I could feel her hands trembling above mine.

"Now!"

She let go, and my hands moved swiftly to replace hers. There was very little loss of blood.

The motel door opened. All eyes swung toward it, expecting paramedics. In walked Tom Canby. "I was driving by and saw all the lights . . . whoa," he stopped. "Am I interrupting something?"

"Just a little emergency medicine." I turned back to the boy. "The ambulance will be here soon," I said. (*It better be.*) "Does it hurt much?"

"Naw," he said with the stoic mannerisms of your typical macho male.

The wait was interminable. Could the ambulances in Bayfield be horsedrawn?

"Can I help?" Tom came close.

"Yes. Bug nine-one-one."

He went to the phone.

"Where are you from?" I asked the boy.

"Vermont."

"Vermont?"

He nodded.

My fingers were beginning to ache. How had Maggie lasted so long? "We don't get many people here from that far away." I sounded like a true native.

"We went to see the president."

"You did?"

"Yeah." He managed a shy grin.

"What did you say to him?" *Come on, damn you,* I urged the ambulance silently. I could hear Tom urging them in stronger language behind me.

"Oh, *he* did all the talking. He gave me a medal. I'm a Scout."

"Wow!" (*Where the hell are his parents?*) "Hey, Tom, did you hear that?" He had hung up on 911. "We've got a real hero here. What was the medal for?" My eyes went back to the boy.

"Nothin'." Again—the modest macho.

"Come on . . ." God, my fingers were killing me. "The president doesn't give medals away for nothing, does he, Tom?" I deliberately drew him with my question, in case my fingers gave out and he had to take my place.

"Right."

"Well . . ." the boy stopped, his eyes fixed on something behind me.

"What the hell have you been up to?" The male voice had the volume of a lumberjack.

I almost relaxed my grip.

"Are you his father?" Tom asked evenly.

"Who do you think I am?" He moved into my line of vision. A bulky man, in flannel shirt and a pair of jeans two sizes too small. His face was a dull red with suppressed rage—or alcohol.

"Sorry, Dad," the boy muttered.

"Your son had an accident, sir." He missed the sarcasm of my *sir*. "He cut himself badly on some glass. We're waiting for the ambulance."

"There's only one ambulance to cover this area," Tom said, repeating what he had just learned over the phone, "and it was answering another call." As he spoke, the faint wail of a siren could be heard. Paul went outside to make sure they didn't miss the motel.

Another wail joined the first. This one was uttered by a small, mousy woman who scuttled into the lobby and slid down next to the boy. "Bryan, baby."

"Don't jar him," I ordered.

She looked at me and then at her husband fearfully. I imagined she spent her whole life looking at people fearfully. The boy edged slightly away from her.

"Don't touch him, Myra," her husband barked.

The sirens, which had been slowly gaining in volume, were now earsplitting. When they ceased, the door burst open and two medics strode in.

"Severed artery above the left wrist," I said.

They relieved me quickly and expertly. I worked the blood back into my fingers.

"Okay," the first medic spoke. "Who's going to ride with us? We can only take one."

Myra looked at her husband.

"I'll go," he said. As he joined the entourage, he shouted at his wife, "Don't come to the hospital unless I send for you."

She nodded dumbly.

"He'll be all right," I assured her. "Those medics know what they're doing."

She smiled gratefully.

I began putting my kit in order. "Too bad about the carpet," I said to Maggie.

"No problem. Nothing that cold water and a little elbow grease won't cure." Spoken like a veteran inn keeper. She led the boy's mother to a more secluded corner of the lobby, where she began talking to her quietly.

"You okay?" Tom asked me.

"Oh, sure." I smiled weakly.

"How about some coffee?"

"Great. Let me get cleaned up first." Some blood had stained my jeans when I'd relieved Maggie.

In my room, I glanced in the mirror and was shocked at my pallor. I changed into a clean pair of jeans and made a feeble attempt to scrub the bloodstains from the old ones. They stubbornly remained. Tomorrow I would give them a bath in Clorox.

When I got back to the lobby, Myra and Maggie were gone. Tom was leaning on the counter talking to Paul. He looked up. "All set?"

I nodded. As he stepped away from the counter, I noticed he was limping slightly.

"What's wrong?"

He shrugged. "I tripped."

"Chasing deer?"

"Sort of." He grinned.

"Serves you right."

When we got outside, he said, "Hope you don't mind riding in a pickup?"

"Compared to my bike, this is luxury."

Despite my protestations, he insisted on walking around and opening the door for me. PC manners (or lack of them) had not yet come to South Jersey.

I liked being enthroned in the truck. It was fun being up high, looking down on all the Munchkins in their toy cars. "It's nice up here," I said.

"I like it." He drove well. Deliberate and sure. Not too fast or too slow.

I was just beginning to relax when he said, "Here we are." He pulled into the parking lot of the most gorgeous blue-and-silver diner I'd ever seen (and I was a connoisseur of diners).

"How did I miss this?" I climbed down quickly before he could come around to help me.

"You were too busy getting lost," he took my elbow, "to have time to locate the best eating place in town."

"THE BLUE ARROW," I read the sign aloud. "I see why it appeals to *you*."

"And it's open twenty-four hours," he said.

"Even on Sundays?"

"Yep."

Would wonders never cease?

It was warm inside and smelled of coffee brewing. He led me to an empty booth. "Hungry?" he asked.

I wasn't until he asked, but something smelled awfully good. Suddenly I realized that, true to form, I hadn't eaten all day. "I guess I could manage a burger."

"Sally!" He signaled the waitress. She seemed calmer, less harried than her New York counterparts.

"The usual?" She smiled at him.

"For me, yes. But this young lady . . ."

He ignored my eye rolling.

". . . will have a burger and coffee."

She turned to me. "Rare, medium, or well done?"

"Medium, please."

When she left, taking the unused menus with her, he said, "I would have pegged you for a rare."

"Looks are deceiving."

"Not when it comes to turkey," he reminded me.

I had the grace to blush.

"What is your usual?" I asked with a gleam in my eye. "Venison?"

"Tell me." He leaned across the table, and his expression was not completely friendly. "Why are deer so much more precious to you than, say, turkeys? Because they're cuter?" He pulled a napkin from the metal container and tossed it at me. "They're both God's creatures, you know."

He had me.

Sally returned with silverware and steaming coffee. This was a high-class place.

"You must come here often," I said, anxious to change the subject.

"Almost every day."

"What do you do, when you're not hunting?" I asked carelessly, not meaning to revive the sensitive subject. But this time he didn't rise to the bait.

"I'm a . . . carpenter."

Involuntarily my eyes dropped to his hands. Strong and brown, one cradled his coffee cup, the other rested lightly on the Formica tabletop.

"That's right." He followed my gaze. "Like you, I work with my hands. But," he smiled, "I don't save lives. Just houses. I refurbish them. Make them habitable again."

"Sounds interesting." With a shock, the memory of a particular old house came back to me. The emergency with the boy had temporarily wiped it from my mind. "I see a lot of old houses when I'm riding around."

"Do you know how old?"

I shook my head.

"The average house around here is pre-Revolutionary. Sixteen-ninety to seventeen-sixty."

"No kidding? I had a lousy teacher for American History. But I can see how it would be interesting when you're surrounded by it."

"Down here you're surrounded by it all the time."

Sally plunked their orders down. His "usual" turned out to be meatloaf and mashed potatoes with coleslaw on the side. My burger was done perfectly. Conversation lagged as we dug in. When we had cleaned our plates, he said unexpectedly, "You were fine back there."

His tone of genuine respect caught me off guard. He didn't know *how* fine. He didn't know how nervous I was with that Boy Scout. And he didn't know my track record with kids. With—one kid.

"Just how serious was it?" he asked.

With a jolt, I remembered he was speaking of Bryan, not Sophie. "If Maggie or I had loosened our grip," I said slowly, "he would have bled to death in a few minutes."

"That's what I thought."

"Actually, this has been an interesting day." Impulsively I described my attack.

His expression ran the gamut from interest, to concern and then outrage. As I came to the end of the story, his brown hands clenched and unclenched on the table as if around the neck of my attacker. "Have you reported this?"

"No. I was about to when I walked in on that emergency."

"What are we waiting for? I'll drive you to the police station right now." He threw down a tip, grabbed the bill, and stood up.

I hesitated.

"What's wrong?"

I remained mute. He was watching me.

"This isn't the first attack."

He sat back down.

"Someone shot out my tire a while ago."

"For God's sake. Did you report that?"

"No. I thought it was an accident. I took it to Mike's garage. You know Mike?" Silly question. Everybody knows everybody in Bayfield.

He nodded.

"Mike told me it was probably just some kid shooting rabbits." I kneaded my napkin into a tight ball. "But now I'm not so sure."

"Come on. Let's go." He stood up. "You can tell the police all about it."

"But I can't." I remained obstinately seated.

"What do you mean?"

"I didn't see his face and I don't know where I was."

He stared.

"Yeah," I admitted. "Lost again."

"But . . . how did you find your way back to the motel?"

"I have no idea." I shrugged. "As soon as he fell off, I turned the throttle up all the way and kept going until I saw the motel sign. I don't know how I got there or how long it took. . . ." I made a zero with my thumb and forefinger.

He shook his head. "What about the house? Any details? Was it brick or wood? Two or three stories? Did it have a porch?"

"Brick. It had a wooden porch. And I think it had three stories."

"Now we're getting somewhere. How about chimneys?"

"Don't know."

"Color?"

"Too dark."

"You said it was set back among some trees and the driveway was overgrown?"

I nodded.

"What about the truck? Make? Color?"

"I think it was a Ford. Same as yours, actually. But I couldn't tell the color. Light gray or white."

"As soon as it's daylight, I want to drive you around the area. This house has to be within a five-mile radius."

"I don't know—it might have been more. I was doing about a hundred miles per hour."

"Well, it's worth a try. I'll pick you up at six A.M. sharp." He got up, and this time I joined him.

With his hand between my shoulder blades, he steered me toward the cash register. As he paid the bill, Sally paused and said "so long" to both of us. But her smile was only for him.

Back in my room, I was still jazzed up from my emotional day. I couldn't sleep and I didn't feel like reading. Rummaging through a drawer, I came across Becca's sketchbook. I carried it to the bed and began browsing through it. Barns, houses, sheds. Barns, houses . . . house! I sat up. There it was. The house. Brick. Wooden porch. Three stories. Trees. Driveway overgrown. But Becca had done me one better. As was her custom, she had drawn it from many different angles. And she had zeroed in on details. There were two chimneys, in which she had meticulously drawn every brick. And a rear view, showing that the ground behind the house sloped down to the river. But the clincher was a side view that showed the owner's initials and a date imbedded in the brickwork: "I & S—1723." For identification, that was as foolproof as a fingerprint or DNA sample. With this sketch in hand, there was no reason why we couldn't locate the house tomorrow.

CHAPTER 31

It was a black-and-white day. Winter, on her annual laundering kick, had bleached the color out of everything. Cornstalks, once a warm yellow, were stark white. The wheat fields, once the tawny brown of fresh toast, were the sickly gray of oatmeal. And the sky, usually a variation of every color of the rainbow, was one solid color—gray. Like gray wool. No—gray clay. Instead of lifting you up, it pressed you down, like a pot lid.

Tom was on time. As I came out, he started to climb down from the cab, but I zipped around to the other door before he could open it. Would he ever learn some manners? Or rather, would he ever dump his old-fashioned ones?

The first thing I did was show him Becca's sketch.

"Who did that?"

I told him.

"This'll be duck soup. That's Israel and Sarah Wistar's place."

"No kidding." I had no idea who Israel and Sarah were.

"I worked on that house a few years ago. But the descendants all died and it was boarded up. I didn't know it was occupied again."

"Maybe it isn't."

He looked at me.

"Well, I've been thinking. Maybe that guy just parked there, waiting for me. I never saw him go into the house, you know."

"That's true." He was thoughtful. "Let's ride over and take a look." He shifted gears and we moved off.

"Dreary day," he commented.

"You're not kidding. It's rare when the scenery around here doesn't give me a lift. But not today."

"How did you end up in this neck of the woods?"

"By accident. I got off the turnpike and landed here. I was so tired, I jumped at the first motel I came to."

"The Oakview Motor Lodge?"

"Right."

"Lucky us."

I glanced at him, checking for sarcasm. There was no sign.

We drove in silence for a while. It was that kind of day.

"We're almost there." He perked up.

I started scanning the side of the road. Sure enough, the familiar driveway, choked with dead grass and weeds, came into view. "Do you think we should stop? What if someone's there?"

"I'll cruise past."

He drove by, neither increasing nor decreasing his speed.

I craned my neck, trying to see up the driveway. The house was shabby. And the windows were all boarded up—something that had escaped my notice in the dark. There was no truck in sight.

"Shall we go back?" he asked.

"I guess. Maybe he dropped something. Or there's some sign of our scuffle."

He made a U-turn. As usual, there was no traffic to worry about. We pulled into the driveway.

I jumped out and started searching the ground. There was a deep gouge where I'd popped my wheelie and dumped my assailant. I bent lower, looking carefully among the bedraggled grass. It was badly trampled, but I found nothing else. After one more scan, Tom suggested we walk around the back and look at the river. On the way, he pointed out the date and initials in the side wall. Intricately worked in blue and red bricks, they spelled out I & S, and under that, 1723, just as in Becca's sketch.

"Wow!" I said.

"You like that?"

"It's fabulous." And I meant it. It sort of gave me goose bumps.

He seemed inordinately pleased by my reaction.

The ground leading down to the river was wet and soggy. My Reeboks and his heavy work boots squished as we walked. There was a thin coating of ice at the edge of the river. Suddenly cold, I shivered. He started to put his arm around me when a noise caused us both to turn.

Two men in psychedelic-orange vests—mandatory hunting gear—stood near the house, staring down at us. They both carried rifles.

I started walking up the slope toward them. Tom followed.

"We were just admiring the brickwork," I said, smiling.

"I worked on this house at one time," Tom said, "and I wanted to show it to my girlfriend." He cast me an affectionate look.

I refrained from kicking him.

"I hope you don't mind?" I said.

The taller of the two men shrugged. But the shorter one said, "This is private property."

"I'm sorry," said Tom. "The place was all boarded up and looked abandoned. We didn't see a sign."

"The house is empty, but we've got permission to hunt on the land," he said. "We wouldn't want you to get hurt." His look expressed the exact opposite.

Unsmiling, they followed us around the house and watched us climb back into the truck.

As we drove off, I waved.

"You shouldn't have done that."

"Why not?"

"Those guys are tough. They might think you were making fun of them."*

"I doubt it. I don't think they have much sense of fun."

"Did you recognize either of them?"

His question startled me. "No."

"Could either of them have been your attacker?"

I considered. "Maybe the taller one. How do I know? I told you I didn't see him. It was dark. And he was behind me the whole time." I was growing agitated. I didn't like the idea of having come face-to-face with my attacker.

"Easy." He placed his hand on my knee. "I didn't mean to upset you. Did you notice the smoke?" he asked.

"Smoke?"

"From the chimneys."

"No."

"I think that house *is* occupied," he said. We drove in silence until we neared the motel. "Shall we go to the police station ?" he asked.

"What would I tell them?"

He was thoughful. "I guess you're right."

I climbed down from the cab. "Thanks," I said.

With a nod, he drove off.

When I walked into the lobby, I had a visitor: Juri.

"Hi," I greeted him cheerfully.

He came up and got right to the point. "Do you have Becca's sketchbook?"

Taken aback, I stammered, "Uh . . . yes," and lied, "She lent it to me."

"I'd like it. Please."

The "please" was definitely an afterthought.

"Sure. I'll get it right away." Actually, it was in my backpack, but I thought I'd better go through the charade of getting it from my room, or he might wonder why the hell I was carrying it around with me.

While I waited in my room for the allotted time it takes to

remove a sketchbook from a drawer, I wondered why Juri wanted it so badly. But more important, how did he know where to find it?

As I handed it to him, I asked, "Have you heard when Becca's coming home?"

"No." Flat and uncompromising.

"Could you give me her Florida phone number?"

He frowned. "They're moving from place to place."

"Well, the next time you talk to them, would you ask Becca to call me?'

He nodded curtly and strode out.

The rest of the day was uneventful. I went to bed early, still exhausted from the previous day's adventures.

When the telephone woke me, the clock beside my bed read 2:15. I groped for the receiver. "Yes?"

"Jo?" It was the barest whisper.

"Who is this?"

A little louder. "Becca."

"Becca? I can hardly hear you. Where are you calling from? Florida?"

"No, I'm . . ."

A strong male voice with a foreign accent spoke sharply in the background.

"Becca?"

We were disconnected.

I punched the operator button.

"Hang up please and dial again," the robot woman's voice chirped.

Trace a call. How do you trace a call? My sleepy brain refused to function. Information? Maybe they'd know. I dialed it.

"Information. How may I help you?"

"I want to trace a call," I said.

"Where are you calling from?" The woman's voice was annoyingly calm.

"Bayfield, New Jersey. The Oakview Motor Lodge. I just received the call a minute ago." I gave her my number. "It's urgent."

"Just a minute, please." Conferring in the background.

Hurry up, for God's sake.

"Was that a local call?"

"No, I don't think so. Florida? I don't know . . ."

"Just a minute, please."

Oh, hell. The whole world could blow up and you'd still be saying, "Just a minute, please."

"I'm sorry, I'm afraid we have no record of your call."

"Shit. Thanks a lot." I hung up. It was only then that I remembered the magic number for tracing calls—★69. But now it was too late. Some detective I was. Now all I could do was pray Becca would call back. But who cut her off?

CHAPTER 32

After Becca's call, I couldn't get back to sleep. What the hell was going on? Where was she? Why did Juri want that sketchbook so badly? I'd been all through it. There was nothing in it but drawings of broken-down barns and old houses. Who attacked me? And why me? Did I know something that I didn't know I knew? Did someone want me out of the way and he was using scare tactics? I went over all the men I'd met at Bayfield. Juri, Mike, Paul, Milac, Jack-the-night-clerk . . . Tom. Then there were my patients. Even more absurd. Of course, it had been a perfect stranger. My attacker was your plain, ordinary, garden-variety rapist. Then why was Becca calling me? Had Juri actually relayed my message that fast? I was under the distinct impression he wasn't going to relay it at all. And why were we cut off? Or were the two things unrelated? That night I discovered the true meaning of the phrase "tossed and turned."

I must have dozed off in the early morning hours, but when I awoke I felt as if I hadn't slept at all. I dragged myself out of bed and took a cold shower. It didn't help. The best cure, I decided, was a quick ride on my bike. Maybe I could find that diner—the Blue Arrow—and have a decent breakfast for a change.

It was a perfect winter day. The grayness was gone. The sky was a cloudless blue and the fields, by some miracle, had been colorized a pale gold. I set off in what I thought was the direction of the diner. Someday, maybe I would learn to pay attention when someone else was driving, and memorize the route for future expeditions.

It was warmer than yesterday. I left my jacket unbuttoned and stuffed my scarf in my pocket. "La dee da dee da. Oh, what a beautiful morning, oh, what a beautiful day . . ." I felt better. The sparkling sign of the Blue Arrow just ahead made me feel better still. I pulled in and parked. My boots rang out cheerfully on the metal steps.

The coffee smelled as good as yesterday. There were empty booths and plenty of vacant seats at the counter. Then I remembered—it was Sunday. Everybody in Bayfield was at church. Sally was there, looking at loose ends with no customers. Tom was nowhere in sight. I took a stool at the counter and ordered eggs, sausage, hash browns, toast, orange juice, and coffee. The mirror across the counter revealed a bleary-eyed woman in need of a good night's sleep. I concentrated on more appetizing attractions: an assortment of scrumptious-looking cakes and pies under a plastic lid; a variety of Danishes; Multicolored toy boxes of cereal nestled in a basket. The enormous, elaborate coffeepot, polished within an inch of its life. And the short-order cook, shoving my hash browns around on the grill while entertaining a regular customer with a description of her high jinks at a party the night before.

Suddenly I was drowned in a wave of homesickness. It was the smell of the hash browns that did it. How many hash browns had my father and I shared? Hundreds? Thousands? My appetite vanished. I got up and started toward the pay phone in the rear.

"Hey, your breakfast's ready," the short-order cook yelled after me.

"Hold it," I said, "I'll be right back."

I went to make my call.

He was thrilled to hear from me. Why hadn't I called before? How was the practice going? When was I coming home? When could he come visit? In my weakened condition, I agreed to let him come for Christmas.

"I've found the greatest diner, Dad. I'm calling from there now. I'm sure they serve a fabulous Christmas dinner."

By the time I hung up, my appetite was back in full force.

As I gobbled breakfast, I pondered all that had happened to me in the past few months. A true New Yorker, I felt more private in a public place than when I was alone. I was able to concentrate better surrounded by noise as long as it had nothing to do with me, such as the cheerful chitchat between the short-order cook and her atheist customer. (He had to be an atheist, or he'd be in church.)

It had begun that first night, when I arrived in Bayfield. Mrs. Milac woke me with her scream of pain. Then she and her husband had skipped without paying me or their motel bill. That afternoon, I'd picked up a waif by the side of the road, put her back, and reported her to the state police. That night I'd had a flat, got lost—for the first time—and paid a visit to Becca's house (before I knew it was Becca's house). As I was receiving directions from the farmer (later known as Juri), a harsh, sexless voice sprang out of the darkness, urging him to send me on my way. The next day, I spotted the Milacs at Mike's garage and gave chase—to no avail. Soon after that, I discovered Becca at the motel, interrupted her adventure with that boy-child, paid my second visit to her home, and was irritated by Juri's persistent questioning of my future plans. Dinner was strained. The next morning Mike informed me that my flat had been caused by a bullet, and unceremoniously presented me with same.

"More coffee?"

"Thanks." I took a long pull of the steaming liquid and went back to my mental journal.

The next few weeks I was totally preoccupied with my decision to move to Bayfield. I spent a week in New York arranging things, and the next few weeks here—putting my room in order and preparing my new office. Then work had begun in earnest. I was busy either seeing motel patients or worrying why I didn't have more private patients. Sometime in the middle of all this my nightmares about the nuclear power plant began.

To assuage my fears, I took a tour of the plant and ran into Milac again. I returned the next day to find that once more he had skipped—this time taking his personnel file with him.

"Would you like anything else?"

"No thanks."

She scribbled the check.

This was followed by The Prune Epiphany The Milacs and the refugee couple at Becca's house were one and the same. Becca's visit to my office to tell me about Milac's rough stuff; Becca's abrupt disappearance and aborted phone call; and finally, Juri. His rudeness and sudden interest in Becca's sketchbook.

I left some change on the counter and headed for the cash register.

It wasn't until I was back on my bike that I forced myself to think about my attacker. (I had a strong tendency not to think about him, I noticed.)

No one could have known I would be coming that way at that particular time. He couldn't possibly have been lying in wait for me personally. The guy was just some horny bastard who had seen an opportunity to lay a lone female in the dark. Or was he? Had someone been hanging around the motel when Paul gave me that message, overheard my destination, and guessed what route I would take back from Delaware? There was really only one. And those detour signs—had they been arranged deliberately to misdirect me past the Wistar house? Or was my attacker merely protecting the property? Those two goons we met yesterday had said the place wasn't occupied. Then why the smoke? Was that beautiful old house being used for something illicit—or illegal? Like making drugs? Or hiding Becca? And her aunt? Had they kidnapped her, too? Should I investigate? Keep it under surveillance? But how? Not from the road. Too obvious. What about the river? No one would notice a small boat in the dark. The trees would screen it from the house. I don't know the river, or how to go about getting a boat. But I could find out. . . .

As I pulled into the motel parking lot, I felt better. I knew I was about to take action.

• • •

Paul told me where I could rent a motorboat. But he also warned me that it was dangerous this time of year. Storms came up unexpectedly. And sometimes there were chunks of ice in the river. He recommended that I wait until spring to explore the Cohansey, when the weather was milder. I nodded noncommittally and went to my room to study my county map—and the river.

I had paid very little attention to the Cohansey River—a name given it by the earliest settlers, Native Americans known as the Lenni Lenapes. Until now, my whole interest had been concentrated on the bay. But now I studied the river with interest. Extremely convoluted, it wound its way through the marshlands like a piece of spaghetti with St. Vitus' dance. At one time Bayfield had been a thriving port. During Thanksgiving dinner, Tom had mentioned that it had been used for smuggling before and during the Revolution. There had been some talk about pirates and buried treasure—Captain Kidd and Blackbeard—which I'd taken with a great big grain of salt. But there was no doubt this river was the perfect way to transport illicit goods, whether tea, flour, Spanish coins—or cocaine and heroin. As I refolded the map, there was a knock at my door.

I opened to Maria.

"No more splinters, I hope."

"Oh, no." She giggled and held up her finger for my inspection. Then she became serious. "It's my mother."

"Is she ill?"

"I don't know. But she isn't herself. She is tired all the time."

"You live with her?"

A look of horror crossed her face. "Oh, no. No one lives with my mother."

"Your father?"

She grinned. "He was the first to go. He left when I was three years old. Then each one of us left as soon as we were old enough."

"I see." I smiled. "Your mother is not easy to live with." Being deprived of my own mother since I was four, I assumed that every-body else's mother was perfect.

Maria raised her eyes to the ceiling. But then her grave look returned. "Still, she is my mother and I must take care of her."

"Come in." I waved her to a chair.

"I can't. I'm working. I just wanted to ask . . ."

"Of course I'll see your mother. When do you get off from work?"

"Three o'clock."

"How about if I meet you at her house at three-thirty? Where does she live?"

"She lives in a trailer outside Bridgeton. But I don't have a car."

"How do you get to work?"

"My husband drops me off on his way to the plant and picks me up on his way home. He has the seven-to-three shift."

The only plant in that neighborhood was the nuclear power plant. "Meet me in the lobby as soon as you're done. We'll go together. You can ride on the back of my bike."

Her grave expression was replaced with delight. "I'll call my husband and tell him not to come."

"See you at three." I closed the door. It was a relief to have the prospect of some work to do. And in the meantime, I could look into arrangements for that boat. I wondered if the rental place was open on Sunday. Paul had given me the number of the Lobster Trap. I dug it out and called.

"Sure. We have plenty of boats. Not much call for them this time of year. What time did you want it?"

I considered. It grew dark about six. "How about six?"

"Sorry. We close at five."

"Can I keep it overnight?"

"Uh . . . that's a little irregular. You're not taking it out at night, are you?"

"Oh, no," I said quickly, "but I want to get an early start in the morning."

"Okay. I'll just charge you for the one day—Monday. That'll be twenty-five dollars."

"I'll be right over."

Except for the greeting of a stray dog, our arrival at the Lenape Trailer Park went unnoticed. Motorcycles were a common sight in these circles. Several trailers had a bike parked in front of them. Maria led the way up the steps to her mother's trailer. It was painted a bright turquoise and had white lace curtains at the windows. From the roof rose a monstrous TV aerial.

A gaunt, elderly woman opened the door, dressed all in black. "Maria?" She seemed more surprised than happy to see her daughter.

Maria spoke to her mother in Spanish. I gathered she was introducing me and explaining the reason for our visit.

"No!" her mother tried to shut the door. But Maria, undoubtedly used to her mother's behavior, had placed her strong, young back against the door. It refused to budge.

In a dramatic gesture, her mother threw up her hands and disappeared inside the trailer.

Not an auspicious beginning. Maria and I quickly followed her in.

The interior was clean and tidy. At one end was a sofa bed and a rocking chair. A small table was attached to the wall that could be raised and lowered when needed. A tiny kitchen, complete with a miniature sink, refrigerator, and stove, occupied the other end of the trailer. Next to the stove was a door leading to another compartment that I guessed was the bathroom. Hand-crocheted doilies decorated all the furniture. On top of the television set, which dominated the entire space, sat an arrangement of plastic daisies. Playing on the screen was a scene from a soap opera in Spanish. (Since it was Sunday, it must have been taped.) It looked like the hero and heroine were about to hop into bed. Maria snapped it off and addressed her mother in more rapid Spanish. When she finished, the older woman waved me into the rocking chair and gave Maria a terse order. The girl went to the sink and began to fill a kettle with water.

Feeling awkward without Maria, I smiled inanely. The woman didn't smile back. She occupied herself with brushing some imaginary lint off her skirt and adjusting her belt until Maria rejoined us.

"Would you tell your mother I'd like to examine her?"

"I already did," Maria said.

I took my stethoscope from my bag and Maria started to unbutton the front of her mother's dress. The woman pulled away from her daughter and proceeded to finish the unbuttoning herself. I decided in this case it would be best to warm the stethoscope. I took it to the stove and held it for a few seconds over the jet of steam emerging from the kettle. I wiped it dry with a tea towel and approached the woman. Although she didn't draw back, she remained stoically immobile while I listened to her heart. It sounded normal. I took her blood pressure. That, too, was within the normal range. I told Maria that I would like to ask her mother a few questions. Taking a history through an interpreter is not ideal; you always missed certain telling innuendoes. I kept my questions to a minimum, sticking to the woman's present condition. Maria could fill me in on her mother's past history later.

The gist of the interview was that the woman had been feeling tired for a number of weeks. She had no energy and no appetite. Such vague symptoms could signify a serious illness or merely indicate overwork or mild depression. In order to make a diagnosis, I would need tests. A chest X ray, a blood count, and an SMA. For these, she would have to go to the hospital. I told Maria this. Maria told her mother.

The woman shook her head vigorously and began to rebutton her dress.

Maria told me, "You make the appointment. My brothers and sisters and I will see that she gets there."

I nodded and packed up my things.

The shriek of the teakettle filled the small space. Maria

jumped up to remove it from the burner. It was essential that we have a cup of tea and cookies before we left, Maria said, or her mother would be insulted and they would have an even harder time getting her to the hospital.

I acquiesced. The tea was very good. And the cookies were delicious. Not store-bought but a lacey, home-baked concoction that melted in my mouth. I smiled at the woman, raised my half-eaten cookie, and smiled again. She understood. When I reached for a second one, she gave me the shadow of a smile.

I shook her hand before I left and said, *"Gracias"*—the only word I knew, other than *si*, in Spanish.

She nodded, but there were no more smiles.

The stray dog was waiting for us outside. He followed us to the entrance, barking all the way.

I took Maria home—she lived in a small apartment in Bridgeton—and went back to the motel. After arranging the appointment for her mother and calling to give Maria the date and time, there was nothing more for me to do. I was forced to think about my evening escapade. It was a wild hunch—that I would find Becca in that house. But I couldn't leave any stone unturned. I couldn't let another child come to harm, I told myself fiercely, without doing everything I could to prevent it. In a moment of weakness, I thought of calling Tom and inviting him to come along. How un-PC. How pre-millennium. Why did I need a man with me? I was young and strong and capable. I even knew how to handle a motorboat. My father and I had often taken one out when we went fishing or crabbing on our seashore vacations, and he had made sure I knew how to operate it as well as he did. No, this was my idea, and I'd carry it out alone. I began to consider what clothes to wear and what equipment to take. The weather was mild for December. I decided on jeans, a sweatshirt, and my parka; a flashlight, my penknife, and bottled water. Maybe I'd better pick up a sandwich at the diner. No telling how long this vigil would last. I couldn't help feeling there was some vast conspiracy going on—in which Becca's disappearance played only a small part. I had mapped out my route on the river. Using the outboard, it would be about a twenty-minute ride. But if I didn't want to be heard, I'd have to row the last lap, and that would take twice as long. Fortunately, the sky was overcast. No full moon to target me for my enemies. Enemies? How melodramatic. But that was how I felt. I felt as if I were going into battle. I wished I were armed. Well, I was, in a way. I had my penknife. I giggled. Part humor, part hysteria. I glanced at Ichabod, grinning in his corner. Was he laughing with me, or at me?

CHAPTER 33

Jack-the-night-clerk was the only one around as I was leaving. He looked up from his latest *Star Wars* paperback. "Hey, where you goin'? Got a big date?"

"Yeah." I winked. "Don't expect me back tonight."

"Right on." He gave me a sly smile.

As I rode to the dock, I felt perfectly comfortable in my sweatshirt and windbreaker. The dock was deserted. Surprise, surprise. Who but a crackpot like me would be stupid enough to take a boat out at night in December? I parked my bike behind the Lobster Trap, well out of sight, and locked the ignition.

The boat was waiting by the dock. The motor caught on the second pull and I eased her out. I had studied the river's course carefully on the map and felt fairly confident as I moved away from the bay and headed inland. Either Tom or Paul had said the river was narrow, but deep. In Colonial times the Cohansey had been trafficked by schooners and clipper ships, they had said.

A huge bird emerged from the reeds to my left, thrashing the air with its wings, scaring the hell out of me. A heron, probably. My eyes had adjusted to the dark and I could distinguish the shoreline easily. My biggest worry was when to cut the motor and start rowing. I didn't want to get too close to the house with the motor on and alert my quarry. Of course, my whole plan would be worthless if this was a night when no business was being transacted and Becca was miles away. I might have to make several visits. The prospect didn't appeal to me.

I had brought a flashlight, but was reluctant to use it except in an emergency. It might attract attention.

I passed a farmhouse with a lighted candle in every window— one of my favorite Bayfield Christmas customs.

A dog barked.

When I had gone about two miles, I shut off the motor. According to my calculations, the Wistar house should be around the next couple of bends. The only sound was the gentle lap of water against the sides of the boat. The stillness was suffocating. Or was it the stench? Because the temperature was above freezing, the smell of decayed fish was strong. I placed the oars in their locks and began to row. I had to stay in the middle of the river to avoid getting stuck in mud. Although the river was deep, its banks consisted of thick, black mud—like tar.

Splash! Something jumped from the bank into the water. A turtle or an otter? I rested my oars, listening. No wind caused even the smallest rustle among the tall reeds. The silence and solitude settled over me like a damp fog. For the first time in a long time, unwanted thoughts surfaced, catching me unawares. During the day, my busy life kept them buried, and at night, exhaustion usually kept those ugly dreams at bay. But here, by myself, in the darkness and the silence of the river, the old film started up—slowly unfolding, image after image. Sophie in the ER; Sophie in her hospital bed; Sophie's parents . . .

Scenes of Becca intruded. Becca on her bike; Becca romping with Elsa; Becca on the porch swing—sketching. What would Sophie have been like at thirteen? Like Becca? Where was Becca? Was she safe? Or had I failed her, too?

I rowed fiercely around the first bend. One more bend and I should see the house. I had better look for cover—something I hadn't given much thought to. I couldn't stay in the middle of the river—a sitting duck for anyone whose eyes were adjusted to the dark. But how could I hug the bank without getting stuck in the mud? I had to risk getting stuck and hope I could free myself later by pushing against the bank with an oar.

As I steered the boat carefully to the right, the house came into view—a dark bulk looming above the sloping bank. No lights. From the third-story windows, there must be an excellent view downriver—in the direction from which I had come. A perfect lookout for pirates and smugglers in Colonial days. Or today. I steered into the bank and drew in my oars. The wall of reeds provided some cover. My luminous watch dial read 8:05. I began to prepare for a long vigil. There were two plastic cushions on the floor. (Did boats have floors?) Positioning myself on the bottom of the bow, I tucked one behind my back, the other under my butt. It wouldn't do to get too comfortable; I might fall asleep and miss the whole show. If there was a show. I reached for my water bottle, pulled out the stopper, and took a long swig. Ugh. Lukewarm. I'd save the sandwich for later. I longed for my Walkman. I'd deliberately left it behind; I had to keep my ears open to listen. For what? A car? A truck? Another boat? Voices?

My boat was lying parallel to the bank, pointing upriver. From my place in the bow, I had an excellent view of the house but not of the river behind me. I was counting on my ears to alert me to anything approaching from that direction. Eyes in the back of the head would have been a welcome accessory. Too bad it hadn't been included in the package. Maybe in the next upgrade. I yawned. My biggest problem now, I realized, was not aquiring another pair of eyes, but keeping the pair I had—open.

CHAPTER 34

Nine-fifteen. I must have dozed off. What woke me were the deep throbs of a heavy motor—much heavier than mine. The throbs were coming from behind me. I turned. A large, shadowy craft was maneuvering the last bend. No lights. Surely an infraction of the coastal laws, but a blessing for me. I lay prone and slithered along the bottom of the boat, humped over the middle seat, and slithered some more until I was able to grab the tarpaulin tucked under the stern seat. The throb of the motor grew louder. I pulled the tarpaulin up until it covered me and lay still, trying not to breathe. Only when I was sure the craft was well past did I lift a corner of the cover and peer out. At the same time my boat was struck by swells from the larger boat and began to rock violently. Some of the waves sloshed over the sides of the boat, wetting me. As the swells died away, so did the throbs of the motor on the big boat. I watched it glide soundlessly along the dock below the house. Either they hadn't noticed my boat, or had thought it was abandoned and not worth bothering with.

A slight stir began on deck, but still no lights. That could mean only one thing: Whatever they were delivering or picking up was illegal. Two figures appeared near the rail, outlined against the faintly lighter sky, and began lowering ropes. One of the two leapt from the deck to the dock, landing as softly as a cat, and began fastening the rope to something (I wished I knew nautical terms) on the pier. Neither spoke. There was the sound of metal scraping against wood. I raised my head a few inches. Another man had joined the one on deck and they were lowering a gangplank. Once in place, the man on the dock ran up the plank and disappeared inside the boat. After that, it was quiet except for the soft lap of small waves against the sides of my boat.

For the first time I was aware of discomfort. The ridges on the bottom of the boat were pressing into my spine, and the water brought in by the swells had soaked through my jeans. I was lying in a pool of water, and it was cold. What did I expect? It *was* December. I should count my blessings. If it had been July, I would have been devoured by mosquitoes.

Somewhere on the larger boat a door creaked. There was a sound of scuffling. A dark object was poised at the top of the gang-plank—waiting to be pushed or carried down. A barrel or a case? No, it was long and thin. It looked like a tube or pipe. Two men ran down the gangplank and waited at the bottom. Two men on the boat began rolling the pipe (if that's what it was) toward them. It made no noise. It couldn't be a pipe. It must be something soft. Like a rug? A rolled-up rug. Were they in the carpet business? What could be illegal about that? Orientals, stolen from Turkey or Pakistan? Another rug quickly followed. Then another. And another. Or was there something hidden inside those carpets? Drugs? Or some other contraband?

A commotion began above on the sloping bank. A man emerged from the back of the house. He was pushing something. As he drew near the river, I made out a hand cart. The kind of device used for bearing luggage at airports and train stations. When he reached the dock the other men began loading the carpets onto the cart. It took four men to lift one carpet. And even then, they did not do it easily. The cart could accommodate no more than two carpets at a time. The ends hung over the sides and it took three men to push it up the bank. Even then the process was frus-tratingly slow. Sometimes a wheel would catch on a root or a stone.

Then they would have to back up and maneuver around it. When they reached the house, they disappeared. There was no light in the house. I could only guess that they deposited their burdens inside. The return trip was much faster. They fairly hurtled down the slope, careless of the empty, rattling cart careening in front of them.

I watched them load the hand cart five times. Ten carpets. When they were done it was 11:45. The operation had taken over two hours. They shoved the gangplank back and the heavy motor began to throb. The catlike man unfastened the ropes (moorings?). He climbed up the side of the boat—without help, it seemed. There must have been a ladder. He was barely over the rail when the craft began to move forward and execute its turn. I ducked under the tarpaulin as the boat slid past and headed back the way it had come.

I decided to give them half an hour before I left. With its powerful motor, the boat should be well into the bay by then. My back was killing me. Shivers racked me at regular intervals. I was chilled through. Could I last the half hour? While I had been watching the men, my mind had been occupied and I had forgotten my discomfort. Now I craved action. Anything to get my blood going again. Pushing my boat out of the mud should provide all the action I needed. I felt a sneeze coming on. By sheer will power I forced it back. I tried not to look at my watch. I told myself stories from childhood: "The Ugly Duckling" and "The Three Billy Goats Gruff." That was my father's favorite. He did the three goats' voices very well.

The tarpaulin jerked off.

In the dark above me appeared a pasty face with the luminosity of the moon. Doughboy—er, Milac.

"Get out."

The harsh order startled a bird. It flew straight up from the reeds and downriver toward the bay. I fervently wished I were him—or her.

Another man came up behind Milac. Great. Plenty of help to

push me out of the mud. "I'm afraid I'm stuck. Could you help push me out?" I asked plaintively.

Neither looked helpful.

"Get out," Milac repeated.

"It's too muddy," I whined. "Why don't you just give me a shove and I'll be out of your way."

He glanced at his buddy. The buddy gave a brief nod. Together they moved toward the boat. I grabbed an oar and shoved it against the bank. It sank deep into mud. I grabbed the other oar and tried to push against the river bottom. That sank, too. Milac was climbing over the bow. Should I jump and swim for it? Swim for what?

The cheerful notes of "Yankee Doodle" rang out. My cell phone. It was stowed in my backpack under the bow seat along with my medical kit—two items I'm never without. Milac paused, listening. Another Yankee Doodle refrain. Locating the source, he dragged my backpack from under the seat. Rummaging inside, he pulled out the phone. For one wild moment I thought he was going to hand it to me.

With a smile, he tossed it over the side of the boat.

CHAPTER 35

"Mr. Nelson?" Jack-the-night-clerk on the phone.

"What's up?" Paul's voice was groggy with sleep.

"A call just came through for Jo. They said she doesn't answer her cell phone."

"Did you try her room?"

"No. I saw her go out. She said she might not be back tonight. Big date."

"Huh? Are you sure she wasn't pulling your leg? Try her room on the house phone. I'll wait."

Jack tried. No answer. He went back to the other phone. "No soap."

"Did the call sound like an emergency?"

"They all do."

"Tell the party to call nine-one-one. And Jack?"

"Yeah?"

"Let me know when Jo comes in."

"Even if it's the middle of the night?"

"You heard me," he barked and hung up.

Jack spent the rest of his shift daydreaming about what Jo could be doing that would keep her out all night.

CHAPTER 36

I woke to the stench of urine.

At first I thought I was back at Camp Minawoski and my tent-mates had locked me in the latrine again. They had done that to me once as a joke when I was twelve, the one and only time Dad sent me away to a summer camp. They didn't get away with it. I threw all their clothes in the lake.

I opened my eyes. Total blackness. Not a slit or a crack of light. No sound either, except a faint moaning to my right. I knew that sound. I had heard it in hospitals often enough. It was the moan of a person in pain. Where the hell was I? In one swift flood, it came back. The boat. The mud. Milac. I must be in that house. The attic or basement? I tried to move my arms. They wouldn't budge. Legs? Same thing. Something was binding me—squeezing me. I felt as if I had been stuffed into a sewer pipe—two sizes too small.

I stopped trying to move and decided to try out my vocal chords. "Yoo-hoo!"

The moaning stopped.

"If someone's in here, speak up!"

Silence.

"Parlez-vous Français?"

Silence.

I cursed my poor language skills.

"Sprechen Sie Deutsch?"

Silence.

"Español?"

That was it—the full extent of my linguistic abilities.

"Sprechen . . ." The word was no more than a whisper to my right. The same direction from which the moans had come.

"Sprechen Sie Deutsch?" I repeated urgently.

"Ja." A woman's voice. *"Bitte."*

I racked my brain for more German words. Something from high school. Anything. Something from the endless Grimms' fairy tales. *Mutter. Grossmutter. Wo?* Where? I wanted to say *Where are we?* but all I could remember was *wo.*

"Wo?" I said.

Silence.

"Wo?" I repeated, louder.

"America," the weak voice whispered.

Great. Wonderful. I want to know where in Bayfield I am. Specifically, in what house and which part of that house? And she tells me what country I'm in. If I hadn't been so tightly bound, I would have laughed. But I could barely breathe.

"Wo?" I tried again.

The voice was weaker this time. I could barely make out the sounds. "U.S.A."

Thanks a lot. I peered into the darkness, trying to see if any of my neighbors were as tightly bound as I was. I couldn't see a thing. How frustrating. How could I expect to find Becca when I was sealed up tighter than a hotdog in Handi-Wrap? Thank God my vocal chords were still intact. "Becca?"

"Hssssss." My neighbors briefly came alive.

"Becca!" If I couldn't rescue her, at least I could let her know I was nearby. Maybe she could take some comfort from that.

Silence.

I lay staring into the dark, inhaling the smell of urine.

CHAPTER 37

I must have dozed off. When I woke, I had a splitting headache and a raging thirst. I decided it was time to call room service. I began to yell. Unfortunately my throat was dry and my yell was not up to its usual emergency-room standards. I tried again.

It wasn't totally ineffectual because the German-speaking woman on my left began hissing, "Shhh! Shhh!"

I yelled louder and was rewarded by the door being flung open and a man's voice: "What the hell's going on?"

"That's what I want to know," I shouted. "And while you're at it, how about a glass of water and a toilet—not necessarily in that order."

He didn't answer right away, stunned, I assumed, by my unorthodox request. Like Oliver's request for *more*.

"We'll see about that," he said ineffectually and shut the door.

The meager light that filtered from the hallway during this interchange had allowed me to make out a long, narrow room under a sloping ceiling. It was lined with mattresses occupied by bodies, either sleeping or pretending to be. The body on my right had actually shot upright when the door opened, but instantly collapsed again. My companions were not physically bound, as I was. Something stronger than bonds were keeping them tied to their beds.

The room seemed darker than before. If nothing happened by the time I counted to one hundred, I planned to start yelling again.

"One, two, three, four . . ."

As I counted, I thought about the door-opener. It wasn't Doughboy. Even in that poor light, his faint silhouette was taller and his voice was different. Younger. And minus the foreign accent. Straight Bayfield country drawl, in fact.

". . . twenty-three, twenty-four, twenty-five, twenty-six . . ."

My bindings were still a mystery to me. When the door opened, I had been so intent on looking at the opener, I hadn't noticed what was compressing me. All I could make out in the dim light was a long tube extending from my neck into darkness.

". . . forty-four, forty-five, forty-six, forty-seven . . ."

A rug.

I was rolled up in a rug—just like the ones I'd seen delivered by that boat!

". . . sixty, sixty-one . . ."—or was it seventy? I'd lost count.

No wonder I couldn't move. I tried a shrug. My left shoulder rose about half an inch. Same on the right. I tried to wiggle my toes. My big toe quivered and died. God, my throat was dry. I was about to let out another yell when the door flew open. A figure paused, silhouetted in the doorway. Shorter and rounder than the first.

"I hope you have my water," I snapped.

For answer, the figure walked toward me. He was carrying something. A bucket. I could just make out two black-currant eyes imbedded in a pasty face before the freezing water hit me. I gagged and spluttered. The worst part was not having my hands free to wipe the water from my eyes and nose. Like a dog, I shook my head from side to side, trying to get rid of as much water as possible. By the time I was breathing normally, Milac was gone. The room was dark again. And still. Not one of my companions had reacted to this assault. It was as if they were dead—or afraid they would be, if they came to my aid.

The only good that came from this incident was that some of

the water actually did make it down my throat. It felt a little less parched. The bad part was, contact with all that water had increased my urge to pee. Soon I would be adding to the stench that already surrounded me.

CHAPTER 38

The door was flung open. Four men came in quickly. Before I could speak or yell, a rag was stuffed in my mouth and a scarf tied over my eyes. I felt myself rise in the air and move forward, still in a horizontal position. There was a name for this, wasn't there? Levitation? I was dimly aware of someone rousing the remaining occupants of the room as the door closed behind me.

I was carried down two flights of wooden stairs. Fifteen steps, I counted, to the first landing. Then fifteen more. At the bottom, I was turned in to what must have been a narrow hallway, because I was tilted almost upright to make the turn. I think I was moving down the hall toward the back of the house. I heard a door open and felt the brush of cooler air on the exposed part of my face. Once outside, I was unceremoniously dumped onto a cart and trundled down a rough incline. The fishy smell of the marsh reached me and I knew we were nearing the river. I had the answer to one question: Where was I? I had been imprisoned in the Wistar house. We stopped with a jolt. Men's voices. Some words exchanged that I couldn't make out. The slap of water against wood. Levitation again, ending in a bruising bump. My destination was not to be stationary. It rocked and swayed under my back. The boat dipped twice in succession, as if from some weight. Two men stepping into the boat, one after the other? The creak of oarlocks.

(No motor?) The breeze on my face increased as we moved off. The only good thing about my swaddling clothes was they would keep me from freezing to death, on this night that was growing colder and colder. Again, the presence of water all around me was having an unfortunate effect. If I had an accident, I fervently hoped the carpet that bound me was a priceless Saruk.

I tried to call up some of my father's words of wisdom.

"There's no free lunch." Not useful.

"Too many cooks spoil the broth." Inappropriate, unless my captors were cannibals.

"Mind over matter." Better.

"A rolling carpet gathers no moss." Ha.

"He who laughs last, laughs best." Since I could barely breathe let alone laugh, this was no help.

I lay awhile, letting my mind go blank, feeling the river rocking under my back. I was sorry about the blindfold. One always likes to check out one's captain and crew before setting sail. But I was even more sorry about the gag. There were a number of things I wanted to say.

"The race is always won in the last lap." The phrase leapt into my head. Not original with Dad, but one of his favorites—and certainly applicable. (Churchill was one of Dad's heroes.) Like the seasoned runner, I decided to conserve my energy for that final spurt. Closing my eyes, I waited for what would happen next.

CHAPTER 39

As soon as the alarm clock went off, Paul reached for the phone and dialed the motel. Jack answered, his voice blurred with sleep.

"Did she come in?"

"What? Who? No."

"Maybe you were in dreamland," Paul snapped. "Call her room." He twisted and untwisted the phone cord while he waited.

"No answer," Jack said.

Ignoring the breakfast Maggie had laid out for him, Paul pulled on his jacket, cap, and gloves.

"Be careful driving," Maggie warned.

As he drove his pickup to the motel, Paul tried to calm himself. Maybe she *had* had a date and decided to stay all night with a boyfriend. What a fool he'd look. As Maggie said, Jo was a grown woman. And young people today were so much freer. God, when he thought of his courtship with Maggie he had to laugh. She had been a virgin—and so had he. He had thought he'd concealed his innocence pretty well until Maggie said, "Where's the instruction manual?"

Pulling into his parking space, he scanned the lot for the motorcycle. Nowhere in sight. No accident had been reported either, he hastily reminded himself. He had been flattered when Jo had asked if she could put his home telephone number in her wallet for emergencies. But he had never expected there would be one.

Jack was packing up his things.

"Did she say anything else? About where she was headed?" Paul couldn't help asking.

Jack looked up. "I told you, she said she had a big date. Then she winked." He gave a sly smile.

That was the first he'd heard of the wink. But that could mean anything. That she really had a big date, or she was pulling Jack's leg. He hung up his jacket and took his place at the desk. He began running up some figures on the adding machine.

"Anything else?" Jack asked.

"No."

He hesitated. "You really worried?"

"Go home and get some sleep."

On his way to the door, Jack turned. "Maybe I should hang around."

"Beat it."

Jack left.

CHAPTER 40

"Hey, Mac. Take a look at this."

The guard left his post at the end of the room full of whirring machines. The operators, intent on their work, did not look up.

"See the buzzards?" He directed the guard's gaze out the window at the field where two large birds hovered above the head of a scarecrow. "Soon one of them will land," he laughed, "and *bingo*! One less goddam foreigner!"

"What did he do?" The guard asked cautiously.

"Stole my cell phone and tried to call home." He scowled. "Stupid bastard!"

The guard drew his breath in sharply. A buzzard had landed on the shoulder of the scarecrow.

"Ha!" The supervisor slapped the guard on the back. "Now we'll have some fun. Gotta see this. Time for a break. A *lunch* break." He laughed again and drew the reluctant guard closer to the window.

CHAPTER 41

At 11:30 Maggie arrived with Paul's lunch. She looked concerned but she didn't say anything. Thank God she wasn't the kind of wife who burbled things like, "Don't worry" or "I'm sure everything will be all right."

As Paul picked at his lunch, he tried to recall everything he could about Jo. Her arrival in that funny outfit—a chic suit with sneakers and a backpack. The way she had come to the rescue of that woman on her first night . . . Suddenly he knew Jo was in serious trouble. She would never leave her cell phone uncovered voluntarily, date or no date. He opened the backdoor to his office, the one that led to the working parts of the motel—the laundry, the kitchen, and a small workshop. "Maggie!" he shouted.

"She's in the laundry, Mr. Nelson." Marie looked up from the sheets she was folding. "Want me to get her?"

"No. I'll go." He pushed past her.

Maggie came out of the laundry bearing a pile of white towels smelling of Tide. "Is she back?"

"No." He looked around furtively and spoke in a low voice. "Remember that couple that was here a few months ago?"

"What couple?" She looked exasperated. Hundreds of couples had been here a few months ago.

"The one with the sick wife that Jo treated."

"Oh, yes." She nodded.

"Put those towels down, for God's sake."

Carefully Maggie laid the towels on a chair. "What's all this leading to, Paul?" She had her hands on her hips. A bad sign.

"They skipped without paying."

"So what's new?"

"It upset Jo. She thought she should go after them."

Maggie smiled at the righteous indignation of youth. "If I could count the number of times people had skipped . . ."

"I know, I know, but she meant well. And she ran into them again at Mike's garage. They drove in for gas while she was picking up her tire. When they saw Jo, they took off."

"Did they recognize her?"

"Why else would they take off?"

"Then what?"

"One day Jo took a tour of the nuclear plant. She wanted to know how it worked, she told me, so she wouldn't be afraid of it."

"Sounds sensible."

"But when she came back, she was all in an uproar. Said she'd seen the husband half of the couple. He was working as a security guard at the plant."

Maggie frowned. "How strange."

"Strange, my foot. It all fits together now."

Maggie was thoughtful. "You mean you think he recognized Jo on the tour?"

"Sure. Why else would he quit?"

"Quit?"

"Yeah. Up and left the same day with no notice. Swiped his personnel file, too."

"So what's your point? Do you think he kidnapped her?"

When put that way, it did sound ridiculous. He shrugged.

"Mr. Nelson?" Marie called. "You have a customer here."

Maggie grabbed her towels and fled.

• • •

Later, when Maggie came to relieve her husband at the desk, she said, "she's still not here! Paul, we have to call Jo's father."

"Oh, God." Paul moaned.

"I'll call him. Do we know his number?"

"No, but I know his name. Joseph Banks. And he lives in Queens." He prepared to leave. "I hate to stick you with this . . ."

"Never mind." Maggie dialed Information with no more fuss than if she were calling the laundry to report a missing shirt—one of the reasons he had married her.

Less than ten minutes later, Paul was back.

"He's going to try to get a plane to Philadelphia tonight," Maggie told him, "and rent a car. I gave him directions."

"Was he . . . ?"

"What do you think? But he seemed in control." After a minute, she said, "We better tell Tom, too."

"Canby?"

She nodded.

"What's he got to do with this?" He was startled by a twinge of jealousy.

"I think he'd like to know."

"But the first time I saw them together was at our house on Thanksgiving. And they hardly spoke. I didn't think they took to each other at all. They aren't dating, are they?" He ran out of steam.

"No. That's not his way," she said firmly. "But . . . he's fallen for her."

"What?"

"Calm down, Paul."

Obediently, he shut his mouth. From long experience, he knew that in matters of this sort his wife was usually right.

"Of course, he doesn't know it yet," she added.

"Will you call him?" Paul asked finally.

"No—I think you can handle that."

"Thanks." He grunted.

Maggie looked fondly after her husband's retreating back.

CHAPTER 42

Paul took off in his truck. He would have gone crazy if he had had to sit around the motel another minute. But he felt guilty. He should make that call. He pulled into Mike's garage.

"Any news of the doc?" Mike's worried face appeared at the window.

Paul shook his head. While Mike filled his tank he went over to the pay phone to call Tom. No answer. Relieved, he went back to his car. He hated to be the bearer of bad tidings. He'd rather Maggie do it.

When he had paid for his gas, he looked over at the pay phone. A bunch of teenagers had taken it over. They'd be there for hours. Well, he'd tried. He drove off, heading nowhere in particular.

Polly had been trying Jo's number all day. She had important news. Becca wasn't in school and the school secretary had no record of Becca's aunt calling to say she was sick. No one answered the phone at Becca's house. Polly hung up. She would try Jo again later.

The Lobster Trap was closed for the winter, except for the small lunch counter that was kept open all year round for the especially hardy sailors and fishermen. Fred Taney, the owner, was chewing the fat with one of those fishermen when his son, Clyde, burst in the door.

"Hey, Dad, did you rent a boat yesterday?"

"Yeah. What about it?"

"It's still out."

"I know. She said she'd probably be out all day." He glanced at his watch. "It's only four."

"Okay. Will you take care of it? I've gotta to get home."

"Whatsa matter, wifey's orders?"

Clyde glared at his father and slammed the door.

Fred and the old fisherman shared a grin. Neither of them had ever let *their* wives tell them when to be home.

"Your girlfriend was in here yesterday." Sally slapped a glass of water, some silverware, and a napkin in front of Tom.

He glanced up.

"She put away a man-sized breakfast," the waitress said.

"Well . . . she's a big girl."

"You like 'em big?" She had a glint in her eye. Sally was solid, but pint-sized.

"I like 'em any way." He grinned. "Where's my dinner?" He made as if to slap her backside.

With a laugh, she scurried away.

In Bayfield you had to play the macho game or they'd think you were queer.

Tom left the diner with Jo still on his mind. He decided to drop by the motel on the off chance he might bump into her. When he walked in, Maggie was at the desk.

"Hi, beautiful."

She glanced up with a frown.

"Something wrong?"

"Jo's missing."

He stared.

"She didn't come home last night. She hasn't been back all day."

He remained quite still. "Did she tell anyone where she was going?"

"She told Jack she had a big date and not to wait up." The expression on Tom's face made her add quickly, "But I'm sure she was pulling his leg."

"Have you asked everyone?"

"Everyone I could think of."

"What about her cell phone?"

"She doesn't answer it."

"And her emergency calls?"

"Nine-one-one's taking them."

He chewed on his lip. "She took her bike?"

"It's not in its usual place."

"Where is Paul?"

"Out looking for her. He's half-crazy."

He slapped the desk. "I'll take a look around."

"Go ahead. But if she doesn't turn up by nine o'clock, I'm calling the police."

Tom checked the clock over the desk: 7:25.

CHAPTER 43

It took Tom less than five minutes to get to the road leading past the Wistar house. (It had taken fifteen minutes when he was with Jo.) He had the presence of mind to pull off the road a good hundred feet before he reached the house and shut off the motor. Silently he slid from tree to tree toward the house. Even though it was a cloudy night, the roof and chimneys were faintly outlined against the sky. No crack of light came from the house. No smoke. And no sign of any vehicles. Clinging to the brick wall, he made his way around the side of the house to the back. Nothing there.

After circling the house, he concluded it was the vacant, boarded-up property it appeared to be. Like so many other houses in the area, it had been abandoned upon the death of the owners, with no living descendents to claim it, and was simply awaiting the erosion of time—or the quicker, more humane death of the bulldozer. He made his way back to his pickup. He had been so sure he would find her here. As he slid behind the steering wheel, he had no idea where to look next.

When he had rushed out, he had had nothing in mind but a driving desire to rescue his . . . his what? His slight acquaintance? A young woman doctor with whom he had spent a few hours and exchanged a few words? Oh, hell, it was his humanitarian duty to find her. She was a doctor. A lot of time and money had gone into her education. He owed it to the human race to see that she lived to practice her profession.

Lived?

He pressed the accelerator.

As he drove, he thought of Jo's friends. The Nelsons, 'Mike,' Maggie's sister, Polly; Jack; Marie; Becca . . . The lights were on full at Mike's garage. He pulled in and Mike came right up. "Any news?"

Paul must have been here. "No. I was hoping you might . . ."

Mike shook his head, wiping his hands on a rag.

"Well, if you do . . ."

Mike nodded grimly.

Tom headed for the Sheffield place. As he drew near, he saw only one light—in a second-story window. Bad sign. If the family were back, there would be more lights. He checked his watch: 8:30. Juri, all by himself, probably turning in early. He pulled fifty yards past the house and parked. His first instinct was to break down the door and search the place. *Easy. No point getting Juri's wind up.* He controlled himself. What excuse could he give for dropping by? He hardly knew the man. They belonged to the same community but had no common interests. He'd met him a couple of times—at the post office and the obligatory fireman's' muskrat dinner. Juri was partial to muskrat. Tom hated it—and the way they trapped them. He wondered if Maggie had already called the Sheffields. He should have asked. He glanced in the back of his truck for something to help him. Nothing there but his bow and a couple of arrows. He grabbed the bow and rummaged in the glove compartment for his flashlight.

There was no bell. He knocked twice. A dog barked. He waited. The barking stopped. He knocked again. More barking, followed by heavy footsteps. Lights came on behind the drawn shades. The door opened and Juri squinted into the darkness.

"Tom Canby. Sorry to bother you. Was huntin' in the field across the way and lost an arrow." His Bayfield drawl grew thicker as he went on. "They're kinda valuable and I'd like to take a look for it. I think it came this way."

"Can't it wait 'til morning?"

"I'm kinda anxious about it." (He resisted saying "shucks.") ". . . And I've got my light." He held up his flashlight. God, what an ass he sounded.

Juri shrugged. "Go ahead, if it'll make you sleep better." He shut the door.

It had been easier than he thought. But what had he actually accomplished? Permission to spend the night trekking through a muddy field looking for a nonexistent arrow.

He began close to the house, shining his light onto the porch, under the porch, into the crawl space under the kitchen. Did he really expect to find Jo there? The kitchen window burst into light. He drew back. Had Juri decided to have a snack? The shade was down and glowed yellow. A narrow crack of brighter yellow edged one side. Hugging the wall, Tom peeped through the crack into the kitchen. *Peeping Tom.* He snorted. A table and three chairs. Juri came into view bearing a bottle of wine and a glass. He set them down and moved out of Tom's line of vision. When he came back he was carrying a chunk of cheese and a box of crackers. Tom turned away in disgust. Had he nothing better to do than spy on some fella's evening snack? He headed for the barn. The door was unlocked but creaked loudly when he pushed it open. How would he explain his presence in the barn? His arrow could hardly have pierced a thick barn door. Maybe the door had been open during the day and—like a bird—the arrow had flown in? Bullshit. He flashed his light over the empty stalls. Apparently the Sheffields no longer kept animals. A pile of tattered horse blankets. The remains of an ancient wagon. The sound of scuffling. He shot his light into the corner, trapping a pair of shiny black eyes. They vanished.

When Tom came out, the clouds had scattered, revealing a three-quarter moon. Clusters of stars crowded the sky. No time for star gazing. He went around to the back of the barn. A rusty tractor, some wooden barrels, a roll of chicken wire. No need for a flashlight now. He headed into the field and stopped. What was he doing? Jo wasn't here. If she was anywhere, she would be in the house—a prisoner in some darkened room. Not likely. Juri had not seemed nervous or angry when he came to the door. A little curious and mildly annoyed; the normal reaction to an unexpected nocturnal visitor. Hardly the attitude of a kidnapper. And he had been perfectly willing to let Tom search his property. Not the behavior of someone who was hiding something. Or someone. Should he knock again with some further excuse? Such as? *How would you like to share your bottle of wine?* As Tom stared at the kitchen window, the shade went black. He headed back to his pickup.

CHAPTER 44

When Tom came into the lobby, he found Paul pacing.

"Any . . . ?"

"No."

"Did Maggie call the police?"

"Not yet."

"What about the hospitals?"

Paul grew pale.

"I'll do it." Tom picked up the phone. The local hospital phone numbers were conveniently tacked to a bulletin board next to the phone. There were only two.

While Paul listened to Tom making his calls, the night of his son's disappearance rushed back to him. That night, he had done the calling. Maggie wasn't up to it.

"Nothing at Salem Hospital," Tom reported over his shoulder.

That night Paul had felt the way he felt tonight—relieved that Nick wasn't in the hospital. But that was before they had found out Nick was nowhere. Missing. Lost.

"Nothing at Bridgeton either," Tom said.

"What about the Delaware Medical Center?" Paul rooted out the Wilmington phone book and gave it to him.

It would have been better if Nick had been in the hospital—or even the morgue. At least then they would know. It was the not knowing.

"All clear at the Med Center." Sensing that his old friend was suffering, Tom left the phone and placed a hand on his shoulder.

"What now?" asked Paul.

For answer, Tom went back to the phone and made another call. "I'd like to report a missing person."

Paul put his head in his hands.

CHAPTER 45

"If you tell me why you were following us, we may let you go."

Compared to the pounding in my head, the voice was no more than the buzzing of a fly. I opened my eyes. Pitch black. I was lying prone, but the undulating motion was gone. I was on terra firma. And I was no longer bound. I could stretch out my right arm to its full length and run into nothing but air. The same with my left arm. My right leg. Left leg.

"And if I don't?" I answered the bodiless voice that seemed to be coming from above me.

"That would be most unfortunate."

Milac, giving an imitation of a grade-C American movie villain.

"In what way?" I prodded. There must be an intercom imbedded in the ceiling.

A sigh, signifying a deep reluctance to convey the bad news.

"Oh, come on, I can take it," I urged.

"While I was working at the nuclear plant, I borrowed some radioactive material. . . ."

A horselaugh burst from me, despite my sore head. "In what? Your briefcase?" (Grade-C spies always carry a briefcase.) "Or did you seal it in your thermos and bring it home in your lunchbox?"

"You may laugh. But we are not as backward in our country as you think."

An especially sharp pain in my head rendered me speechless. It also gave me time to reconsider. Maybe I'd better not be so flip. If I wanted to survive and find Becca, I'd better keep my wisecracks to myself.

Milac went on. "This material is invisible and odorless, so you will not know when it has been released."

Oh, please . . . It was an effort to contain my groan.

"In fact, you won't have any reaction to the material for two, maybe three years. Then you may begin to lose a little hair. . . ."

Was this guy for real?

"Some bruises may appear on your skin and you may develop leukemia. But you are a doctor; I do not need to tell you the symptoms of leukemia. You know it usually begins with severe headaches."

I swallowed.

"All you have to do is tell me what you are looking for, and all this unpleasantness can be avoided."

I stared at the ceiling (not seeing it), and forced my voice to sound flat and expressionless. "I was looking for Becca."

"Ah, the Sheffield child. What did you want from her?"

I raised my head. "I didn't *want* anything from her. I wanted to see her. She's my friend."

"She's a child."

"A friend, nevertheless."

"Americans have strange relationships."

"It's not a 'relationship,' goddamn it!" I sat up, shouting at the dark.

"Please, don't get excited," the voice above me purred. "Take it easy, as you Americans say."

Go to hell, I thought—but didn't say. I lay down and closed my eyes. My head was killing me. All that shouting.

"I will let you rest."

My eyes flipped open. Could he see me? Did the little rat have a spy hole? Was I under constant surveillance through one of those infrared lenses that spies use to see in the dark? I had seen a window display of those gadgets in a store in Manhattan. They had fascinated me, but I had never supposed I would be on the other end of one.

"While you're resting, you might like to think about the effects of radiation. Perhaps you can recall some stories of the survivors of Hiroshima."

Would he never shut up?

A faint click, then blessed silence. But only for a moment. Into the silence filtered a soft, cloying music. The kind of music that is inflicted on you in department store elevators or over the telephone when someone puts you on hold. A type of music I particularly loathed.

Bastard! I thought, but didn't yell. If I was going to survive and find Becca I had to keep my mouth shut.

The Muzak kept coming.

Was it strange to be fond of a girl less than half my age? I shook my head violently. Dirty-minded little bastard. What did age have to do with friendship?

Becca was a smart-assed kid who needed guidance and a goal. She had no parents, for God's sake, and was being raised by an aunt who was living on another planet and a cousin who was—at best— a question mark. No wonder she was acting out. Under that tough-guy exterior was a lost little girl. . . .

"Holy crap!" I sat up. *You're getting maudlin, Jo. Face it. Becca is a brat. But . . . a brat worth saving. If I can only find her. . . .*

CHAPTER 46

I must have fallen asleep, despite the Muzak. (Because of it? I refused to credit those foul notes with anything.) My dreams, strangely enough, had been happy ones—of my father and me at the seashore, of riding my bike under a brilliant sky, and finally, jumping the waves with Becca—and Sophie. Each child held one of my hands. Suddenly we all three merged into one and were floating on top of the waves, looking up at the sky, and . . . I woke up. To reality: One dead. One missing. One in prison.

But my head felt better. I could think more clearly. How could I have fallen for that radioactive shit, even a little bit—except that my resistance was low, because I hadn't eaten or drunk anything for hours, maybe days. They couldn't possibly risk killing me slowly, over a period of two or three years. I was on to their whole immigrant-smuggling scheme, for God's sake. All those poor people imprisoned in that airless attic with little food or drink and nonexistent sanitary conditions. And God knows what other horrors they were subjected to. No, when they got rid of me, it would have to be quick. Meanwhile, they would try to get as much out of me as they could. Find out how much I knew about their operation, and how much I had spilled to others.

"Good morning, Doctor."

The voice jarred me. Morning. At least I could get my bearings. This must be the day after I rented the boat, unless I had slept for an entire day and night because of some drug they had given me. (Maybe that was why my head ached!) If the boat wasn't returned, the people I'd rented it from would start to wonder, wouldn't they? Maybe even start looking for it? For me?

"Not talking today? How unfriendly. And I thought you put such a high premium on friendship."

Premium? The rat had a good command of the English language. Friendship? Where *were* my friends? Had they missed me yet? Had they begun to search for me? Don't they serve any food in this rat-hole? "I'm hungry," I said mildly.

"If you cooperate, I promise you a good breakfast."

His accent was barely perceptible, like the hint of some seasoning I couldn't put my finger on.

"Why did you follow me to the nuclear plant?" he asked.

Since when do people follow a skunk? "I took that tour because I wanted to know how the plant worked, in case it ever sprang a leak or was attacked by terrorists and I might have to treat the victims."

"Such nobility."

I let that pass. Discussing "nobility" with a sewer rat was my idea of nothing.

"And what about that day at the gas station?"

I had to think a minute. Oh, yeah, I had a big ulterior motive that day. "I was picking up my tire."

"And what about the day you tailed us to the Sheffield farm?"

"*Tailed* you? I was driving along, enjoying the scenery, until I had a flat . . . Wait a minute. It was you who took that potshot at me!"

"Not at *you*. At your tire."

At least one piece of the puzzle fell into place.

"So," he continued, "you maintain that appearing in our vicinity so frequently was a twist of fate? A mere coincidence?"

I hope you don't think I'd actively seek out your company! "That's right."

"And when you came to dinner at the Sheffield's—that was also a coincidence?"

"Of course."

A long pause. I thought he had left until he said, "I hope you find your accommodations satisfactory?"

I swallowed my normal response. "I could use a glass of water."

He didn't answer. Suddenly the room blazed with light. I shut my eyes. There was a grinding noise. My eyes opened to see part of the cinder-block wall in front of me begin to separate from the rest. Through the crack, a hand emerged holding a glass of water. As I grabbed the glass, I tried to hold on to the hand. It slipped from my grasp. Another grind and the crack disappeared. It had been a woman's hand.

I drank the water down in one gulp. Guess that radiation material hadn't arrived yet, otherwise he wouldn't let his wife come in here to wait on me. Unless, of course, he'd grown tired of her. "And I could use a toilet."

After a few moments, the cinder blocks parted again and a portable potty—complete with toilet paper—was shoved into the room. As I scrambled to use it, I wondered briefly if he was watching me. But the call of nature overcame my modesty.

"Anything else I can do for you?" His voice purred with sarcasm.

The little rat—he *had* been watching. "Let me out of here," I said. Now that I could see my living quarters, they appealed to me even less. A small cinder-block cell painted a dull gray. The only furnishings: a cot, the potty, and me.

This time the silence continued. He really had left.

CHAPTER 47

Maggie was on desk duty when Mr. Banks arrived. If she had been asked to describe him, she would have thought a minute and said, "If you put a wig on him, he'd look just like one of those signers of the Declaration of Independence." Maybe it was the glasses—round with steel rims. No, it was the eyes behind them. Clear blue, a shade lighter than Jo's, but just as steady.

"I'm Joe Banks." He came straight up to the desk. "Any news of my daughter?"

She shook her head and swung open the little swinging door that separated the office from the lobby. "Please come in, Mr. Banks, and have some coffee."

He looked swiftly around the lobby as if searching for someone to give him a different answer. His gaze switched back to Maggie. He stepped inside.

"Everything's being done." She poured coffee into a Styrofoam cup. "Cream or sugar?"

"No, thanks. What's being done?"

"The police are scouring the neighborhood. All the hospitals have been contacted and no accident involving a motorbike has been reported—"

"Motorbike?"

"That's how she gets around, makes her house calls. . . . Didn't you know?"

"No."

Maggie felt she had put her foot in it.

"Where was she headed?"

The force of his gaze made her want to look away. She didn't. "No one knows." She wasn't about to repeat Jack's story.

"May I see her room?"

"Of course." She reached behind her, lifted a key from a hook, and handed it to him. "I'm afraid I can't leave the desk. Just take the stairs outside the door and turn right at the top."

"Thank you."

She hadn't realized, until she watched his receding back, how small he was—a good three or four inches shorter than his daughter. Jo was about five foot ten.

When Mr. Banks returned to the lobby, Maggie had gone and Paul had taken her place. Maggie had described him, but Paul would have known him anyway because of his eyes. Paul came out of the office and offered his hand. "Mr. Banks—Paul Nelson."

They shook hands.

"I'd like to register," Mr. Banks said.

Paul took down a key and handed it to him. "On the house," he said.

"No."

"Please."

He pocketed the key. "I'll get my bag."

Paul watched him go. When he reached the door, Mr. Banks turned. "I lost my wife, Mr. Nelson. . . ." His hands clenched at his sides. "I can't lose Jo."

"I know," Paul said. "I lost my son."

The color left the man's face.

Paul dropped his gaze and cursed himself. Maggie would never have said that.

Shaking his head as if to shake off Paul's words, Mr. Banks went to get his luggage.

CHAPTER 48

"Sorry, Canby. We have no authority to search either of those properties. What makes you think she's there?" The police officer was slumped in a swivel chair in front of a computer monitor displaying six playing cards, faceup. From a corner of his mouth hung a dead cigar. The office reeked of dead cigars.

Tom told him about Jo's attacker.

"Jesus!" He leaned forward. "Why didn't she report it at the time? These reports long after the fact are almost impossible to follow up."

Tom nodded. Why hadn't she reported it? Why hadn't he insisted on it? He thought about insisting on anything with Jo. You would probably end up in a fistfight. Or a wrestling match. (Not an unpleasant prospect.)

There was the sound of footsteps in the corridor. The door opened and Paul Nelson walked in with a stranger in tow.

"Any news, Charlie?" Paul didn't even notice Tom.

The officer shook his head and looked at the stranger.

Paul turned. "This is Mr. Banks, the missing girl's father."

"What are you doing to find her, Officer?" Banks went up to the desk.

He did not resemble Jo in stature, Tom noted, but his voice had the same cadence, only deeper.

In response to Banks, the policeman sat up straighter and placed his cigar in the ashtray. "I have an officer cruising the area. We only have two cars, and one has to be on call in case of emergencies."

"What else?"

"We've called all the hospi—"

"And?"

"Nelson here said he and his wife called all her friends. . . ."

"I don't think the people she's with are—friends." Tom stepped forward.

"What do you know about her?" Banks's voice had a sharp edge.

"Nothing, sir." He met his gaze. "I wish I did."

The urgency in Tom's voice caught Banks's attention. He addressed his next question to him. "What do we do now?"

"Sit by the phone and wait," drawled the policeman.

"That's not enough," Banks snapped back.

"What about her old friends in New York?" the policeman asked, suddenly happy at the possibility of shoving the whole business on someone else. "Any old boyfriends?" He leaned on the word.

Banks was caught up short.

Tom looked at him sharply.

"She did have a beau," said Banks slowly. "Ken Lawrence."

"Address?"

"I don't know."

"That should be easy, then." The policeman had regained the upper hand. "There can't be more than a couple of hundred Ken Lawrences in Manhattan and the surrounding boroughs. Any other friends who might know the whereabouts of this guy?"

Tediously, they followed the Ken trail to its logical conclusion. A series of phone calls eventually established that Ken had been in Denver on a business trip during the time of Jo's disappearance, with plenty of witnesses to testify to the fact. When they finally reached Ken himself, he offered to come down to Bayfield. But Banks heard the reluctant tone of his offer and stalled him. "No, thanks. I'll let you know the minute we find her." As he replaced the receiver he looked around the room helplessly.

Tom, who had fidgeted throughout the old beau quest, touched his arm. "Come on," he said, "I've got my pickup. Let's cruise around."

"I'll cover the phone back at the motel," Paul said, inadequately.

Retrieving his cold cigar, the police officer went back to his card game.

"Where are we going?" Banks sat forward as Tom started the motor.

"There's this place I've been watching."

"Why? Does it have something to do with Jo?"

"She was attacked there." Jo's father was clearly not the kind of person you lied to. Tom felt the older man's eyes on him in the dark. "Last week, she stopped at this place to ask directions. She was on her bike and someone jumped her. He tried to wrestle her to the ground, but she managed to stay on the bike, throw him off, and get away."

Banks's sigh was a mixture of relief and exasperation. Tom had a sudden vision of a ten-year-old Jo arriving home late from an extended bike ride, pigtails flapping, knees and elbows skinned and bleeding, to face a father sick with worry. He liked Banks.

CHAPTER 49

The thing that bothered me most wasn't the solitary confinement, or the lumpy cot, or the glaring lights, or the meager rations, or even the primitive bathroom facilities.

It was the feeling that I was being watched.

I didn't know if I could pick my nose or scratch my crotch without being seen. As a result, I did neither. Not because I was afraid of offending my captors' sensibilities; I knew they had none. If they were watching, though, it would demean me in my own eyes and cause me to lose my self-respect—an important commodity to a prisoner.

The intercom had remained silent for what seemed forever. I was beginning to lose my sense of time again. They had removed my watch, of course, as well as my other few personal possessions. (Since I had come to Bayfield, I had begun carrying a small penknife and a hemostat in a pocket of my jeans.

There were no windows. I had no way of telling if it was day or night. I guessed I was well into my second day as a prisoner, but I wasn't sure. There was a period when I had been unconscious that I couldn't account for. I had no idea how long I'd been out.

I had eaten two meals, if you could call them that—the first a bowl of soup that may have passed in the vicinity of a chicken once, and the second a sandwich made of two soggy slices of white bread decorated with a microscopic layer of peanut butter, and a cup of tepid tea.

For some reason I wasn't hungry.

Most of the time I lay on the cot, facedown, eyes closed, trying to blot out the bright lights. In retrospect, the darkness had been more friendly. At least in the dark I could pretend I was hidden from their prying eyes.

I was still dressed in the clothes I had worn when I left home: T-shirt, jeans, socks, and sneakers. I felt filthy. One more discomfort to add to the list. Two days without a shower really bothered me. And my teeth were furry.

Next, I assessed my physical condition. Tired, weak, lethargic.

Ohmygod! I sat up. What's the matter with me? Didn't I tell all my patients after surgery—or after any illness "Get moving!" The old days of enforced bed rest had proved to be disastrous for the human body. I jumped off the cot, stretched, and began to do situps and pushups. Then, like all prisoners before me, I paced my cell.

Counting my steps, I discovered the dimensions of my prison. Ten by fifteen feet—a little bigger than my office waiting room, a little smaller than my motel room. I was examining the hairline crack in the cinder-block wall when a familiar voice startled me. "Did you enjoy your nap?"

I twitched like an eel on a hot griddle, and cursed myself. But it wasn't my fault; it was a reflex that I had no control over.

"Perhaps your rest has cleared your head and you will be more reasonable."

Don't count on it. I had hoped the rat would greet me with the time of day, as he had once before. The reference to a "nap" might mean it was afternoon. I didn't answer.

"You're being very foolish."

Oh, cut out the Hollywood crap. I've seen all those old movies. You can't hold a candle to Claude Rains or Sydney Greenstreet. I stared at the ceiling, willing his round doughy face to appear there so I could spit in one of his black-currant eyes.

As the silence lengthened, I thought of my friends. Where were they? Had they missed me yet? Paul, Maggie, Jack, Mike? Marie, Polly . . . Ken? Shit. I hadn't thought of him in weeks. What would he do in this situation? Quote some stupid poet or philosopher? Dad? Had they notified him yet? I couldn't think about him. Then there was Tom. He would know what to do. He'd probably have me out of here, if he knew where to find me. Or if he cared. I hadn't done much to make him care. In fact, I'd pushed him away. Why? Because—*flash of insight*—after Sophie, I'd anesthetized myself, and it hadn't worn off yet.

"I'm still waiting."

"What?" I came back to the cell with a jolt.

"Why were you spying on us from that boat?" His voice had lost its coy playfulness.

"Spying? I wasn't spying. I was exploring the river."

"At night? In December?"

Chacun à son goût. "That's right."

"You force me to apply different methods."

Oh, spare me the grade-C stuff, I thought. At least stick to high-class films, like *Notorious* and *Casablanca*.

Click.

When he left, my bravado left with him. I began thinking about the "methods" they had used in those old Saturday matinees. Toothpicks under the fingernails. Cigarette burns. Electric shocks to obscure parts of the body. *Stop it!* I forced my brain to make a ninety-degree turn. The power of positive thinking. How had other prisoners kept up their courage, retained their sanity in solitary confinement? I ranged through my meager reading. *The Count of Monte Cristo, The Arabian Nights. . . .* (The thought of sitting up 'til dawn spinning tales for Doughboy—made me nauseous. Luckily, it wasn't an option.) Then there was *The Birdman of Alcatraz.* But this hole had no window. That ruled out bird nurturing á la Burt Lancaster. Once I had read a story in *Reader's Digest* about a prisoner from World War II. He had occupied his mind by playing

CHAPTER 50

It was midnight when Tom pulled into the Blue Arrow Diner with Banks. They had explored Bayfield, to no avail. The house where Jo had been attacked was as silent as the grave. Visits to her usual haunts—Harry's Bar and Grill and now The Blue Arrow—had also proved fruitless. Wearily, they took a booth and ordered bacon, eggs, toast, and coffee. They ate in silence. Not an awkward silence; the silence of two comrades bound by a common cause who felt no need to talk.

Banks paid and Tom didn't argue. When he dropped Banks at the motel, he said, "I'll pick you up at seven. We'll make the rounds again—in daylight."

Banks nodded and climbed down from the cab. Tom waited until he disappeared inside before turning his truck toward home.

Paul was restless. He didn't understand how Maggie could sleep so peacefully beside him. He kept racking his brain for some hint Jo might have dropped, some clue that would help them find her.

"The boat!" He sat up.

"Paul?" Maggie's voice was groggy.

"The boat, Maggie." He shook her shoulder.

"What boat?"

"She asked me where she could rent one."

"When?"

"About a week ago." He switched on the light and fumbled for the phonebook.

Maggie sat up and squinted at the clock: 1:30. "Fred won't be there now."

"I'm calling his home." He began to dial.

CHAPTER 51

I had developed a routine. I would walk around my cell twenty times. Then I would sit down on my cot (not lie) and try to name all the muscles of the body. Then I would take another walk and try to remember all the bones. Another walk—the nerves. Sometimes I would give a lecture to a class of first-year med students on the cardiovascular system. The endocrine system. The nervous system. At least when I got out of here I could apply for a teaching job. Finally, I would invent an imaginary patient with a set of symptoms and diagnose them. I had just diagnosed a middle-aged woman with severe hypertension when the cinder-block wall groaned and separated. In walked the gruesome twosome. Hubby in the lead, wearing a white coat that was an exact replica of my own. Wifey in the rear, bearing a tray covered with a towel—once white, now soiled around the edges. Wifey removed the towel, revealing an assortment of surgical instruments that, under other circumstances, could perform miracles. Hubby began to pull on a pair of plastic gloves. It was a laborious process, pulling the plastic down over each pudgy finger. He would never have made a surgeon; the patient would have died before he got his gloves on. When they were finally in place, he looked at me the way a cat looks at a mouse.

I jerked my knee up under the tray, scattering the instruments across the floor. They made a loud clatter on the cement.

CHAPTER 52

Tom slept poorly. As soon as the first light filtered into his room, he was up, showered, dressed, and in his pickup. A low mist hovered above the fields and road. He flicked on his headlights. The single caw of a crow was the only sound that disturbed the stillness.

He parked at the far end of the Sheffield farm, away from the house, near the riverbank, and stepped into the field. He wasn't sure what had drawn him here. Nothing rational. Just a hunch. If anyone stopped him, he would say he was looking for that lost arrow. He was familiar with the fields and felt at home in them. When he was younger he had been known as a "walker of the fields" by the locals—the name the Indians gave to the men and boys who searched the fields for artifacts. After much practice, the walker acquired a knack for spying arrowheads, shards of pottery, broken bits of clay pipe that worked their way to the surface of a newly plowed field—especially after a rain storm. Tom had quite a collection.

It had rained last night and the ground was soft. If he had been looking for artifacts, he would have found them. But this morning he had something else on his mind. He stopped when he saw footprints. Two deep sets, made by man-size workboots, each pair spaced about six feet apart, as if their owners had been carrying some burden between them. A heavy burden, judging from the depth of the prints. They came from the direction of the river. He followed them, careful to keep to one side and not damage them. They led him across the field to the barn. He entered. After the open field and sky, the darkness closed around him. He felt his way past the stalls, the ladder to the loft, the broad stone trough that had once held grain, and tripped over a bump on the floor. Turning on his flashlight, he saw a metal ring. He reached down and pulled on it, hard. Nothing happened. Then it dawned on him. If the ring was attached to a trap door, he was standing on it. Duh. He moved to the left and pulled again. This time a square section of the barn floor rose. Dimly, he made out steps leading down into darkness, an even deeper darkness than the barn. Holding his light in front of him, he started down. The steps bottomed out on the rough dirt floor of a passage—not much wider than his body, and not as tall. Head bent, he edged forward until the passage dead-ended at a wall. Or a door? He played the light over its surface, searching for a knob, a lock, a keyhole. Nothing. He looked again, this time running his hand around the edge. There. This time he felt a bump. Something round and hard, like the plastic button at the back of his laptop—the one that turned it on. He pressed it.

With a groaning sound, the door, wall, whatever, began to turn inward. A thread of light no wider than a fishing line, appeared to his right. He watched it grow wider.

Under the blazing lights stood an empty cot. On the cot lay a tray. Scattered on the tray were some surgical instruments—and on the floor, a bloodstained towel.

CHAPTER 53

Tom burrowed his way back through the narrow passage, climbed the ladder, and ran to his pickup. His mind racing, he had no memory of driving to the motel. A lone figure stood in the parking lot, looking up and down the road. Banks. Tom glanced at the dashboard clock: 7:15. The older man was waiting for him. Christ, what was he going to tell him? He screeched to a halt and turned in.

"I thought you forgot," Banks said.

"I had an emergency."

"Oh?"

"Get in. I've got to make a phone call. I'll be right back." Tom left him and went inside. The lobby was empty—the office was closed. He called 911.

Banks had barely settled himself when Tom hitched himself into the truck.

"What's up?" Banks stared at him.

"I have an idea." He drove fast, without speaking. At a sign reading "LOBSTER TRAP—ONE MILE," he turned left and followed a dirt road, toward the river. Through a screen of tall, shimmering reeds, the ramshackle wooden building that housed the restaurant came into view. Behind the restaurant rose a cluster of sailboat masts, the hulking bows of a few cabin cruisers, and the water. With a spray of gravel, Tom parked in front of a small weather-beaten outbuilding with a sign—LIVE BAIT—hanging in the window. Inside, two men were conferring over the counter. As Tom and Banks came through the forest of fishing rods, gas cans, and life preservers, one man looked up.

"Fred's lost a boat," Paul said.

"The doctor rented it," Fred added, "and didn't return it."

CHAPTER 54

In a borrowed boat, Tom and Banks started upriver. The mist had evaporated but the sky was heavy with dull clouds, reflected in the water. Tom had the motor at top speed, now that he knew his destination: the Wistar house, where Jo had been attacked. *Of course, that's where she would have headed. On some mission of her own, she had planned a sneak attack, a rearguard action. And, of course, she had to go alone. Some macho woman's code?* Sitting quietly in the stern, Banks demanded no explanation, and Tom offered none.

They passed an abandoned rowboat. Jo's? Tom didn't stop to investigate. They reached the house in fifteen minutes (as opposed to Jo's forty-five.)

The dock was deserted. No one was in sight outside the house. Tom moored the boat and sprinted up the slope, with Banks following more slowly. The boarded windows of the house stared blankly at them. No smoke rose from the chimneys this morning.

Tom pounded on the backdoor. The time for pussyfooting was over. No answer. They went around to the front and did the same. If he had come in his pickup instead of a boat, he would have had his tools with him to pry open the door. Frustrated, he kicked it.

Banks bent to examine the doorknob. He withdrew a contraption from his pocket that contained all the common tools necessary for daily living, from penknife to corkscrew. Applying a screwdriver, he had the doorknob off in seconds. Tom was impressed. They pulled open the door and gasped as the odor of human filth—garbage, urine, and feces—swept over them.

Because the windows were boarded up, the only light came from the open door. After a few minutes they were able to make out the rooms. A living room, dining room, and kitchen on the first floor. The first two rooms were empty, except for piles of trash— old newspapers and garbage. In the kitchen, chicken bones, orange peels, eggshells, and coffee grounds clogged the sink, and the sticky linoleum sucked at the soles of the men's shoes with each step.

Tom was the first to mount the stairs. From the landing, a long room stretched out, filled with heavy-duty sewing machines for stitching canvas or leather. "What were they making here?" he wondered aloud.

Banks came upstairs to have a look. Familiar with printing machinery, he made an educated guess. "Belts, wallets, or handbags, probably," he said.

Tom continued up the next set of stairs to the attic. Another long room. This one had a sloping ceiling and rows of filthy mattresses. At one end was a bathroom. The sink and toilet were stopped up. He had to hold his breath against the stink.

As Tom started down the stairs, he met Banks coming up. "Nothing there," he reported.

Nothing significant turned up in the closets or basement, either. The two men stepped outside and inhaled the fresh air greedily.

"The bastards flew the coop," Tom said.

Back in the boat, they started upriver. After skirting several docks, Tom cut the motor and coasted silently toward shore. There was no dock here, just a wooden post with a metal mooring. As the boat bumped against the bank, Tom stood up and examined the muddy ground. The footprints were undisturbed. He pointed them out to Banks.

"What do they mean?"

"I think Jo went to the Wistar house by boat. They discovered her and brought her here—to the Sheffield place." He waved at the field above them. "They unloaded her and kept her prisoner."

"Where?"

"In an old bomb shelter under the barn." He started the motor and made a U-turn.

"But who . . . ?" Banks cried over the noise, his face white.

"That's what I mean to find out," Tom screamed back.

With a sudden spurt, he headed downriver. This time when he came to the abandoned rowboat, he took a closer look at the faded stenciled letters on its side: PROPERTY OF LOBSTER TRAP. Fred would be glad to know his boat was found.

CHAPTER 55

As they walked to the pickup, Tom noticed Banks was dragging. He glanced at him. He didn't look good. He must be pushing seventy. Tom dropped him at the motel, promising to keep in touch. He watched the older man cross the parking lot with slow, unsteady steps. *He's aged ten years in a few days*, he thought.

Although what he wanted to do was scream and yell and smash things, Tom cruised silently. *Be cool*, he told himself. *Think logically. Now's not the time for hysterics.* Why was he upset? What was she to him? She wasn't even polite. Hell, half the time she was downright rude.

He hardly knew where he was driving when the Sheffield farm came in sight. A police car was pulling out of the driveway. At least they had answered his call. He slowed and waved the car to a stop. Dan, an old high school buddy, was at the wheel.

Tom got out and went over to the window. The policeman cracked it open an inch. It was cold.

"What do you make of the place?" Tom asked.

"Not much to go on."

"What about the bloody cloth?"

"Yeah. It's in back." He tilted his head toward the gray metal container on the backseat. Dan hadn't been the sharpest guy in their class.

"Going to get a DNA?"

"Yeah. I'm gonna drop it off now. Want to come along?" Bay-field cops were lonely. Since there were only two of them, they weren't allowed to travel in pairs.

"No, thanks. But I think the blood belongs to Jo Banks."

"The missing doc?"

"Yeah." Must be one of Dan's brighter days. "You might want to get the name of her doctor in New York. Get her blood type. Maybe even a sample. See if you can make a match. Her father's at the Oakview Motor Lodge if you want to ask him anything. But if you ask him about the blood type, be sure to say it's just routine," he warned.

"Right." Dan rolled up the window.

Back in his truck, Tom continued driving. DNA tests were good, but it took time to get the results. When he was out of sight of the Sheffield farmhouse, Tom parked and got out. The cornfield on his right was still Sheffield property. He shivered, looking at the long rows. On impulse, he plunged into the cornstalks. They crackled and scratched as he bored his way between the rows. It felt good, smashing through the razor-sharp stalks. At least he was doing something. This was an ideal hiding place. No one would think of looking here. He pushed on until he came out the other side. Without a pause, he turned and pushed his way back between the next two rows. He continued until he had covered half the field and came to the scarecrow in the middle. Time to take him in, if they wanted to use him next season. He raised his eyes from the straw man to the leaden sky. Empty, except for two buzzards circling. "God, Jo! *Where are you?*"

A small movement at the base of the scarecrow. The wind? There was no wind. An animal? But there was no sound. Even a mouse would make a rustle running through these dry stalks. He stared at the scarecrow's right foot. Had it twitched? *Get hold of yourself, buddy!* His eyes moved up the faded denim overall, over the shabby gingham work shirt, to the cloth bag tied at the neck with a piece of clothesline. His hat had been lost to the wind long ago.

The painted face, faded after a season in the weather, still wore the ghost of a smile, mocking him. *What are you doing out here, jackass,* he seemed to say.

Tom pulled out his penknife. With a jerk he cut the cord. Yanking the bag upward, Jo's head lolled forward.

CHAPTER 56

He lowered her gently from the pole—she had been hung by her overall straps—and cradled her in his arms. As he bored though the cornstalks, he pressed her face into his chest to protect it from the razor-sharp edges.

He lifted her onto the passenger seat of his pickup. "There you go," he whispered. "You'll be okay now." He propped her, limp and unconscious, into a sitting position, and ran around to the driver's side. He drove with his left arm, the other around her waist, and forced himself to drive slowly in order not to jar her. Even so, her head bounced against his shoulder. He tried to pretend they were at a drive-in movie. "This is a great picture, hon. Pretty soon this car chase will end and we'll get to the love scene. . . ." His voice petered out.

At the emergency entrance, he parked and stretched her out on the front seat. He ran into the emergency room and came back with a paramedic pushing a gurney. The medic transferred her expertly to the gurney and pulled a blanket up to her chin. Tom told him where he had found her.

"Shock and exposure," the medic said, and trundled her quickly inside.

Tom followed until they disappeared into a booth and the medic pulled the curtain.

A businesslike voice spoke at his elbow. "Do you have her insurance card?"

He turned. "What?"

"Her insurance card. We need it for billing—"

"Billing?"

"It's the hospital rule," she said crisply.

"Listen." He leaned into her office cubicle, enunciating every syllable." She doesn't have her card because when she went out three days ago, she didn't know she was going to be kidnapped, tortured—and *almost killed!*"

Everyone paused—orderlies, nurses, doctors, patients. The woman who had asked for the card cowered behind her desk.

"Oh, shit." He walked out.

CHAPTER 57

As soon as he was outside, he knew he couldn't leave. He had to be near her. He moved the pickup away from the emergency entrance and found a parking space. He sat there, his mind empty, unconscious of the cold. Gradually, something nudged at the back of his mind. He got out, hunted up a pay phone, and found one in the lobby.

"Oakview Motor Lodge," Paul answered.

"I found her."

"Is she . . . ?"

"She's . . . in good hands. I'm calling from Bridgeton hospital. Is Banks there?"

"In his room."

"Tell him to get down here. Better have somebody drive him. He was looking a little shaky. Oh, and tell him to go to her room and see if he can find her insurance card."

"Right."

CHAPTER 58

"Dr. Banks is in here. But you can only stay a few minutes." The overbearing voice broke into my dream. It had been a good dream, too. Dad and me walking along the beach, looking for seashells. . . .

"Jo?" A small, cautious voice.

I opened my eyes.

A huge bunch of russet chrysanthemums hovered at the edge of my bed, and above them—a small russet head.

"Becca?"

Her eyes danced. "I knew you'd make it!" She threw the flowers on the bed and reached for me.

I was dozing off again when I felt a familiar hand resting on mine.

"Dad?"

He couldn't speak. His eyes glistened as he squeezed my hand.

That evening, they came in pairs, bearing their blue visitor cards, allotting them five minutes apiece. First the Nelsons. They were happy to see me, but subdued, distracted—as if something, nothing to do with me, was preying on their minds.

Next came Maria and Jack. Smiling shyly, Maria placed a package in my hands. I started to open it, but asked her to do it for me. The smallest activity was still an effort. Inside was a small leather-bound Bible.

"The Lord's words are in red," she stammered.

I had paid scant attention to the Lord. Maybe it was time to start. "Thank you, Maria."

"Hey, Jo." Jack stepped forward. "That must have been some date!" He grinned.

"Huh?"

"Don't you remember what you said the night you left?"

"Oh, yeah." I smiled. "Some date." I shuddered.

"Here!" He pushed a flat package into my hand.

"What's this?"

"A video of *The Return of the Jedi*" He grinned. "Watch it with your boyfriend—when you're feeling better," he added.

"Thanks, Jack. I will." I laid the package carefully next to the Bible.

Mike and Polly came together. An unlikely couple. Probably paired by a hospital volunteer. They sat stiffly in their chairs, one on either side of the bed.

"How's school?" I asked Polly.

"Fine."

I turned to Mike. "How're you making out at the garage?"

"Okay."

Small talk was never my forte, and in my weakened condition I was glad for the five-minute curfew. I'd make it up to them later, when I was feeling stronger.

After they left, an aide came to fill my water jug and plump my pillows. The beginning of the nightly routine. "Lots of visitors," she remarked.

"Yeah." I sighed.

"Tired?"

"A little."

"There's one more lurking in the hall. Shall I send him away?"

"Who . . . ?"

"Tall, dark, and . . ."

Tom poked his head in the door.

Oh, God. Was I up to this?

He didn't come any further. Just stood there in the doorway, sort of drinking me in. The aide looked from him to me, and edged around him, out of the room.

"How do you feel?"

"So-so."

He came up to the bed, peering at me. "You look better."

"Than what?"

"Than hanging from a pole."

I laughed. It was the first time.

He sat down. After a minute, he said, "I came to ask you for dinner."

"Sorry. No appetite."

"Not now. When you're out of here." He looked morosely around the room.

"Okay." He'd saved my life, for God's sake. Everyone said so. Becca, Dad, Maggie, Paul—they'd all said if it weren't for Tom . . . Besides . . . I felt my blood stirring like it hadn't stirred for months. "I don't know how to thank—"

"Shh . . ." He placed a finger to his lips. "I'll pick you up at the motel when you're released."

"You make it sound like prison."

"Well, isn't it?"

"Not when you've been in prison."

He looked distressed.

Mustering the last of my energy, I said cheerily, "It's a date."

As he backed toward the door, his smile was the same as that first day, when he forgave me for scaring away his herd.

CHAPTER 59

I later learned that my visitors had been instructed by the doctor
not to tell me too much in the beginning. But gradually, as the days
slipped by and I regained my strength, my friends became less cautious and the story leaked out. From Tom, Paul, and Maggie, I was
able to put together the pieces.

Juri, Becca's cousin, had been the originator of the plan. Having a liking for luxury and a dislike for work, he had always
sponged off one relative or another. When he learned that some of
his Czech countrymen yearned to leave their semidepressed home-
land and come to America—the land of plenty—his scheme crys-
tallized. Because of his aversion to employment, he enlisted the
help of a couple, two former Communist spies (now unemployed),
to take care of the details. Apparently, they made out like bandits. If
Juri questioned any of the Milacs' practices, he was silenced easily
with a bigger piece of the take. The émigrés were lured here under
the guise of free passage to New York and the promise of employment when they arrived. Their passage was free all right, but the
accommodations left something to be desired—crowded together
in the hold of a leaky freighter, with next to no sanitary facilities,
on a starvation diet. When they arrived in New York Harbor, they
were transferred to a smaller boat that carried them to a remote
part of South Jersey—Bayfield. There they were rolled up in car-

pets, unceremoniously dumped at an old farmhouse (the Wistar house), and forced to work in a sweatshop making elegant leather handbags until their captors extracted enough money ($20,000 apiece) from their relatives back home to pay for their cruise and lodgings. If they rebelled or if their production rate fell, they risked my fate—becoming a scarecrow. The dead man that Jake Potter had stumbled on in the field was an émigré from Slovakia who had committed the sin of trying to call home.

One day, Juri discovered Becca's drawing of the Wistar house in her sketchbook, and decided she was getting too nosy. He convinced her aunt to take Becca to visit her grandfather in Prague. "He's getting on, you know." Later, when he found the sketchbook missing and deduced that I had it, he informed the Milacs, and they took matters into their own hands. They already suspected me of spying on them; this merely confirmed their suspicions. I foiled their first attempt to kidnap me by dumping my attacker that night at the Wistar house. But later, when I took the boat upriver, I walked right into their hands.

I still shied away from thinking of my captivity and the persuasive methods they had used to discover my motives. Hollywood does a poor imitation. They know an American audience would never put up with the real thing.

The worst revelation came from Maggie. She had fallen into the habit of dropping by in the afternoon to keep me company until dinnertime. (Dad always ate dinner with me.) Sometimes we talked, but more often I dozed and she sat by the window, knitting. Once, when I opened my eyes, I noticed a tear sliding down her nose. My first thought was for myself, egotist that I am. Did she know something about my condition that I didn't?

"Maggie?"

She brushed the tear away and looked at me.

"What's the matter?" I asked.

She looked away.

I am going to die, I thought. They fudged the tests, lied about the reports. As a doctor, I knew that *feeling* better wasn't necessarily a sure sign of recovery. No use beating around the bush. "Am I cooked?" I demanded, using the medical profession's jargon for terminally ill.

To my relief she smiled. "Oh, no, Jo."

"Then . . . ?"

"Nick . . ."

"You found him?"

She nodded.

"But that's wonder—"

She shook her head.

"Is he ill?"

"No." She lay her knitting aside and haltingly told me the whole story. Her son had been working for the Milacs. Nick was the foreman in the workshop who guarded the émigrés. The job earned him enough to feed his drug habit.

"But . . ."

"Yes." Her mouth formed a grim line. "During those three years while we were mourning him, he was in Philadelphia, just fifty miles away, and for the last six months he's been working a few miles down the road!"

I could think of nothing to say.

"Where is he now?"

"They arrested him. He's in prison, awaiting trial. That handy-man at the Sheffield place—"

"Juri?"

She nodded. "He dreamed up the whole scheme. I didn't even know he knew Nick but he kept in touch with him, and when the Milacs came he contacted Nick and brought him back to run the sweatshop."

I wondered if Nick was the one who had jumped me. My neck tingled and I felt the pressure of those hands on my throat again. "Have you seen him?"

She nodded, turning back to the window.

"And?"

"When we came in . . ." She paused. ". . . he . . . spat on us."

I waited a long moment. Finally I asked, "And the others?"

"All in prison. The FBI finally came in on it. Although it was Juri who dreamed up the scheme, you'll never guess who carried it out."

"Mrs. Milac."

"How did . . . ?"

"She was the one who worked on me. Her husband began the job, but he chickened out, and she took over."

"Oh, Jo . . ." Her eyes strayed to my bandages. "Well, if it's any satisfaction, they're both in federal prison, charged with espionage. He took that job at the nuclear plant to try to find secrets to sell to our enemies!"

I almost laughed. Once a spy, always a spy. But when it came to the Doughboys—er, Milacs, I'd lost my sense of humor.

"And the émigrés?"

"They were sent to New York—to the immigration authorities. They'll probably be sent back where they came from."

Sadly, I thought of the woman on the mattress next to mine who had spoken a little German.

The aide came in with my dinner. As she set down the tray, Maggie began to gather up her things. "I'll be going now."

"Wait." I slid out of bed and hobbled toward her. As I hugged her I could feel her body trembling. I realized I was holding a third Maggie. Not Mrs. Santa, not Mary Poppins, but—Judas's mother. Whoever she was. Nobody ever talked about her, or *her* feelings. But I had been browsing in my new Bible. Maybe I would find her.

CHAPTER 60

One day I had an unexpected visitor: Becca's aunt. Dressed in a mauve suit, black-and-white silk scarf, and chunky gold earrings it was amazing she had made it from the farmhouse to the hospital without attracting a film crew.

"How are you feeling?" She drew a chair up beside the bed.

"Better, thanks."

"We've all been so worried."

Not certain who the "all" included, I let that pass.

"I . . ." She looked around the room as if for help, then continued in an abrupt burst, "I wanted you to know . . . Becca and I didn't . . . we were completely ignorant . . ."

"I know," I answered.

"Actually, you were part of the reason I took Becca to Prague," she said. "After talking to you, it occurred to me if she was going to be an artist, she should see her native city, one of the great art centers of the world."

"But what made you take off so suddenly?" I asked.

Avoiding my eyes, she said, "I suspected those people . . . They weren't like any of the other visitors we'd had. They were furtive and . . . churlish. I told Juri I didn't care for them. He accused me of being a snob. Then one day I saw Becca give the man a fright-

ened look. I took things into my own hands. I updated our pass-
ports, ordered plane tickets, and packed our bags. At the same time,
Juri suddenly got the idea into his head that Becca should meet
her grandfather. 'He isn't getting any younger,' he said. So it
worked out very well. He actually helped us leave. He drove us to
the airport."

"Why didn't you tell Becca ahead of time?"

"I didn't want to worry her. I knew she wouldn't want to leave
school. I thought I had better surprise her."

"I stopped by that same evening," I said. "Juri told me you had
gone to Florida."

"Florida? I wonder why he said that?"

"I don't know."

"Juri wasn't really involved, you know," she assured me. "He is
selfish but he isn't—evil."

I kept my mouth shut.

"He told me he had backed their plan because he thought it
was a way to help his countrymen come to this country—"

"Illegally," I couldn't help inserting.

"Well . . . but I don't think he knew that." She drew a deep
breath. "But I didn't come to talk about Juri. I came to apologize,
and beg forgiveness on behalf of Becca, Juri, and me . . ." Her eyes
wandered to my bandages and looked hastily away. She continued,
". . . for your suffering." She reached for my hand.

I clasped it. "I never blamed you or Becca," I said.

"And Juri?"

Was it so important that I exonerate her cousin, too?

She countered my silence with, "But he didn't know . . ."

I released her hand. That was asking too much. If she wanted
to kid herself that her cousin, boyfriend, whatever was innocent
until the trial was over, that was okay. But I wasn't going to help
her. "Thank you for coming," I said, changing the subject. "Becca
has been a faithful visitor. I hope it hasn't interfered with her
schoolwork."

"Oh, no." She smiled. "Becca's a good student. To tell you the truth I'm glad she has something to do after school besides hang around with that sulky boyfriend of hers."

"Randy?"

Our eyes met and we laughed.

"I've found a local artist who is going to give Becca drawing lessons," she said.

"Great!"

"He's a painter of some note and he was very impressed with Becca's skills."

At this point a nurse came in to take my blood pressure. The aunt seemed to feel this was a natural time to end her visit.

"By the way," I said, as she rose to go, "What is your name? I know you only as 'Becca's aunt.'"

"Ema," she said. "With one 'm'."

Of course. Emma with two "m's" would be ordinary. With one "m" it was romantic—even exotic. "Come again, when you have time," I said sincerely. I *had* enjoyed her company. "Becca tells me you write poetry. Maybe you could bring some for me to read."

She brightened visibly. "I will."

During Becca's next visit, I asked her about the phone call.

"I wanted to tell you about Prague. It was so awesome! And I just picked up the phone and called you. But Grandfather came in, and when he found me calling long distance without permission, he was angry. He's very strict and old-fashioned . . ."

Too bad he lives so far away, I thought.

". . . So I hung up," she explained.

"I was very worried," I said. "I tried to trace the call."

"You did?" She looked pleased.

"You're a pain." I cuffed her lightly on the arm.

"Do you really think so?" She seemed positively delighted.

"Get out of here!"

Instead, she stretched out at the end of the bed, being very careful to avoid my sore feet, and began to conjugate French verbs for tomorrow's vocabulary quiz.

CHAPTER 61

The morning of my release, Dad came to the hospital in Paul's pickup and drove me home. As we entered the parking lot we passed my motorcycle, parked in its usual spot. This was reassuring. Someday I would ride again. Who had retrieved it for me, I wondered? Paul? Tom? We went straight to my room, but our progress was slow. To my chagrin, I had to use a crutch to get up the steps one at a time and lean on Dad as we walked down the corridor. It was my feet. The Milacs had done a job on them. Loaded with nerve endings, they are one of the most sensitive parts of the body.

My room looked good. The Dufy sparkled. Someone had removed Ichabod. Paul, probably. I hoped he had dismantled him gently and laid him to rest in peace. His clothes were stacked and folded in a neat pile at one end of my futon, my tattered gray Columbia sweatshirt topmost. I grabbed it, pulled it on, and curled up under my comforter. Scanning my bookcase, the worn copy of *The Wizard of Oz* caught my eye. I would never read it with the same relish. In fact, I would probably never read it again. My children, if I ever had any, would have to settle for *The Secret Garden* or *Treasure Island* until they were old enough to read for themselves.

Dad stood uneasily, shifting from one foot to the other. He looked older. I hadn't remembered him looking so old. He needed to get back to work. He didn't do well without work.

"It's time to go, Dad," I said gently. "Your print shop is waiting. So are your customers. If you don't go soon, you won't have any customers."

"But . . ."

"I'll be fine. I have good friends."

He nodded. He'd met them. "That Canby fella . . ."

"Yes?"

"He . . ."

"I know. I owe him." I wished he'd go. I wanted to be alone. But I felt guilty about it.

He came over and planted a kiss on my forehead, the way he had every night when I was a kid. "Come see me as soon as you feel up to it."

"Sure," I said, as I always did. But this time I meant it. I reached up, indicating I needed a hug. When he released me, he took a last look around the room, as if wanting to remember every detail.

The door closed.

With a sigh, I reached for the TV remote and turned on the soaps.

CHAPTER 62

I was happily engrossed in the climax of an episode of *General Hospital* when the phone rang. "Damn!" I reached for it.

"Hungry?"

I thought a minute.

"We have a date," he reminded me.

"At the Blue Arrow?"

"No." Pause. "Every now and then I like to branch out."

He saved your life, remember? "Okay, let's branch," I said. "Should I dress?" In Bayfield, going out to eat was a big deal. Some women even wore skirts.

"No. The place I have in mind is very laid back."

"Great."

The fact that I let him help me into his pickup shows I was still convalescing. We didn't talk much, but the silence wasn't unfriendly. He drove over long, flat roads that stretched to nowhere. South Jersey specializes in such roads. The sky stretched to nowhere, too. I'd missed the sky. It was good to be out. Out of the hospital. Out of the motel. Under the sky.

"Juri's in jail," Tom said. "Along with Nick."

"And . . . the Milacs?" I spoke their name carefully.

"In custody, awaiting trial." He cast an anxious glance my way. "You'll have to testify."

"My pleasure," I said between clenched teeth.

"Did you know Mrs. Milac was once a mule?"

"Come again?" I had better names for her from the animal kingdom.

"In the past, she exported drugs to various destinations in her abdomen. She packed the drugs in plastic, then placed them inside the prunes before swallowing them. The prunes helped the drugs go down easier and also helped bring them out faster at the other end."

"Yuck!"

That explained the ugly scar on her tummy. Drug traffickers were not into cosmetic surgery. That might explain her illness, too. Crab cakes and prunes are probably not a good mix. "Dad went back to New York," I said, changing the subject.

"And Paul went back to church."

"You're kidding."

"Nope. Last Sunday he took the plunge."

"Maggie must be happy."

"She's ecstatic. Served him roast beef on her best china, even though it wasn't a holiday."

"What made him go back? Certainly not the return of his prodigal son!"

Without taking his eyes off the road, he said, "You."

"Me?"

"We had a few beers to celebrate your recovery, and . . ."

"I hope it was a high-class brew."

"Heineken. And he told me you had restored his faith in . . ." He swerved to avoid a rabbit. ". . . goodness," he finished.

I let out a low whistle.

"That bad, huh?"

Was he grinning? "Well, I never claimed to be Goody Two Shoes." He *was* grinning. I felt a blush coming on. "Becca's back in school," I blurted, "and on her way to becoming a famous artist . . . or architect. Prague blew her mind."

"And you?"

"And I'm—about to become what I always wanted to be."

"And that is?"

"A famous, humble country doctor." I stole that line from Linus, of *Peanuts* fame.

"Oh, yeah." He chuckled. "I saw your picture."

The Bayfield Press had dug up a snapshot of me on my bike, scarf flying. The headline read: LOCAL DOC BREAKS SMUGGLING RING.

"By the way, where are we?" I sat forward, looking around. When you're in the hospital you give up, let other people take charge. I was ready to end that.

"Don't worry. *I* never get lost."

I let that pass. A small frame house popped up on the horizon. After a minute, we slowed and turned into the driveway. Not a driveway by suburban standards; more a hole in the tall grass.

"New restaurant?"

"Famous for home cooking." He turned off the ignition.

"You cook?" I asked, as he helped me down from the cab and handed me my crutch.

"Every now and then."

"What's on the menu? Venison burgers?"

"They're delicious, by the way," he said maliciously.

I didn't respond. By now I had learned how destructive deer could be and that the county was overpopulated with them. I stared at the house. From a distance it didn't look like much, but up close I could see the work that had gone into it. There was a long screened porch. Perfectly plain—no fancy gingerbread that would need painting every other year. No porch furniture in sight, but I could imagine sitting out here in a rocker on a summer night, watching the lightning bugs bump against the screen. The floor of the porch was made of rough-hewn boards, polished, stained, and coated with something durable to protect it from the weather. A pile of cut logs was stacked in one corner. "You have a fireplace?"

"Sort of." He opened the porch door into the kitchen. Although it had big windows, it was toasty warm. A wood stove, perched on a raised brick platform, was the source of heat. I sniffed.

"Apple wood. You can't beat it for scent."

The warmth and the scent enveloped me. "Let's eat here." I slipped onto a wooden chair next to a window overlooking an empty field. The field was white, although—to my knowledge—it hadn't snowed. "What . . . ?

"They're back." Tom came to look. "Snow geese. They were feeding here yesterday, but I thought they'd gone south."

"I thought they were seagulls," I admitted. I still had a lot to learn.

"Want to see something spectacular?"

"Not if it means getting up." I was surprised how tired I was after spending a day doing nothing.

He grabbed both my hands, pulled me up, and half-dragged me to the base of a flight of crooked stairs. The steps were stained and polished like the porch. He half-pushed me up them.

"How old is this place?" My voice sounded hollow in the stairwell.

"Not old. 1892. It was a tenant farmer's house. Story goes . . ."

I didn't hear the rest. I had reached the top.

There was only one room up here. Large and square with huge windows on all sides. It was like standing in the cabin of a ship. But instead of blue water, I was surrounded by white fields. The winter brown of the fields was completely hidden by the snow geese. As we watched, the geese rose as one—in a single white sheet.

I gasped, "How do they do that?"

"Fly?"

"No, smart guy. Take off all together."

"Nothing to it. The head goose gives a toot. A kind of bugle call."

I continued to stare at the geese trailing south in a V. The last rays of the sun caught their white underbellies, illuminating them like strings of Christmas tree lights. Then they were gone. The field was brown again and twilight wrapped the house in violet.

"What are you thinking about?"

"The Chrysler Building."

He laughed.

"No, seriously. Every night at this time, its lights come on—six jagged arcs. When I'm in Manhattan I try to find a spot where I can see it. After the Twin Towers went, it became an evening ritual. I used to check every night to make sure it was still there. Forty-second and Fifth is the best view. But Thirty-fourth and Lex'll do."

"I thought the Empire State was the big attraction."

"For tourists. The view *from* the Empire State is good. But the view *of* the Chrysler Building is better."

"Homesick?"

I looked at him. "I guess I am."

"Why did you leave?"

I glanced at him sharply.

His return glance was equally sharp.

I turned away with a shrug.

He grabbed my shoulders.

"A child died. It was my fault."

His hands dropped to his sides, but he held my gaze. "What happened?"

I told him about Sophie.

He walked over to one of the big windows and stared out. There was nothing to see now but darkness. With his back to me, he said, "We all have something."

I waited. But he offered nothing more.

"My boyfriend told me it wasn't my fault. That I should forget it."

"Your boyfriend was wrong. There are some things you never forget. You carry them to the grave." He went on in a dull tone. "You may bury them for a while, but they'll jump out at you when you least expect it. . . ."

Like when I saw Becca jump on her bike, grinning back at me. Sophie. Becca.

". . . and the older you get," Tom continued, "the more of this baggage you carry around."

This wasn't what I wanted to hear. But I suspected he was right. And I sensed he was speaking from experience. Someday maybe he would tell me about his baggage.

"That's why people are bent over when they grow old," he added.

"No, it isn't. They have osteoporosis."

His laugh broke the somber mood. "Are you still taking Becca to New York?" he asked.

"Sure. As soon as I can walk."

His gaze strayed to my feet, encased in a pair of oversized bedroom slippers. He looked away. "May I come?"

"Have you ever been?"

"Once. Class trip."

"What did you see?"

"The usual. Empire State, Statue of Liberty, Brooklyn Bridge."

"What did you like best?"

"The bridge. No contest."

"You can come."

I turned, scanning the simple room. Whitewashed walls. A couple of rag rugs. A bureau—rescued from a flea market, probably, and redone, carefully, lovingly. A small table with a single lamp. And a mattress tossed in the corner, covered with a worn patchwork quilt that looked like the real thing. Bachelor quarters, country style. "Is that where you sleep?"

He nodded. "Like to take a nap?" He looked concerned.

For answer, I shuffled past him, dropped onto the mattress, and stretched out, facedown.

"Like it?"

"Too hard."

"Not for a bowman." He slid his full length down beside me.

I looked up. "Did you hear what happened to the bowman?"

"No. What?"

"He got fired."

"Why?"

"He was caught knapping." I giggled.

My reward was a quick smack on the butt. Next thing he knew, I had him pinned to the mattress in a hammerlock.

"Hey! I thought you were convalescing?"

"You should see what I'll do to you when I'm fit."

"I'd like to." He grinned.